Hidden World

Hidden World

Graham Masterton

severn House

This first world edition published in Great Britain 2003 by
SEVERN HOUSE PUBLISHERS LTD of
9–15 High Street, Sutton, Surrey SM1 1DF.
This first world edition published in the USA 2003 by
SEVERN HOUSE PUBLISHERS INC of
595 Madison Avenue, New York, N.Y. 10022.

British Library Cataloguing in Publication Data

Masterton, Graham, 1946-
    Hidden world
    1.   Horror tales
    I.   Title
    813.5'4 [F]

    ISBN 0-7278-5962-5

Typeset by Palimpsest Book Production Ltd.,
Polmont, Stirlingshire, Scotland.
Printed and bound in Great Britain by
MPG Books Ltd., Bodmin, Cornwall.

For Wiescka

Cries in the Night

They caught her as soon as she came out of the art-room door. There were five of them – Sue-Anne, Charlene, Micky, Calvin and Renko. They came rushing down the corridor, howling and whooping and swinging their schoolbags around their heads.

'It's Gimpy!' screamed Sue-Anne. 'Show us how you run, Gimpy!'

'Yayy, Gimpy!' echoed Charlene. 'Dot one, carry one! Show us how you run, Gimpy!'

Jessica backed against the wall, clutching her art portfolio. Micky danced around her, tugging at her bunches. 'What you been drawing today, Gimpy? Fairies and elves? Why don't you never draw nothing but fairies and elves?'

'She's off with the fairies, that's why,' said Calvin.

Renko flicked Jessica on the tip of her nose with his finger; when she raised her hands to protect herself he snatched her portfolio away from her.

'Give me that!' she gasped.

Renko held it out to her and then snatched it away again. 'I just want to see what you've been drawing, that's all. I'm an art lover!'

'More like a fart lover,' Micky put in.

Sue-Anne stood on tiptoe like a ballet dancer and teetered around and around with her hands held over her head. 'Look at me, I'm Jessica and I'm a little fairy!' Suddenly she started to hop grotesquely on one foot. 'Or I would be, if I wasn't such a gimp!'

'Give me back my drawings,' Jessica insisted. 'Please, Renko, that's my whole year's work, practically.'

'I told you,' said Renko, 'I just want to take a look. I happen to have a thing for fairies and elves, you know?'

'Please, give them back.'

'So what are you going to do if I don't?'

'Are you going to tell Ms Solomon?' said Sue-Anne.

'Are you going to cry-y-y?' said Charlene.

Renko offered Jessica the portfolio again, and again whipped it away from her. He took it to the top of the staircase and unclipped the fasteners.

'Renko, no!' Jessica pleaded, limping after him.

'What are you worried about, Jessica? Don't you know that fairies and elves can fly?'

'Don't!'

But Renko tipped all of her artwork down the stairwell – all of her drawings of fairies flying with swarms of bees and humming-birds, her watercolor paintings of elves building villages out of twigs, her sketches of corn-cockle flowers, meadow-pinks and shooting stars.

They twisted and sailed down three stories, scattering on the stairs and the floors below, and as they did so Class III came in from the snowy schoolyard, with their scarves and their gloves and their dirty wet boots, and started to trample on them without even realizing what they were.

'My drawings!' Jessica shouted down to them in panic. 'Don't tread on my drawings!'

One or two of the children looked up, but at first they didn't understand what she was trying to tell them. Then Billy Muñóz looked down and saw that he was standing on her best drawing – a fairy castle, with spires and turrets and spider's-web walkways, and scores of fairies promenading on the battlements. Billy nudged Dean Schmitters, who was standing next to him, and very deliberately wiped his boots on it, smearing the pencilwork and crumpling up the paper.

'No! Stop! No!' Jessica begged him. Behind her, Sue-Anne mimicked, 'No, stop, no, you're squashing all my little fairies!' and Charlene said, 'Now she *is* going to cry!'

Jessica grasped the handrail and hobbled down the stairs as fast as she could.

'Hey, look at the gimp go!' laughed Calvin. 'World downhill speed record for gimps!'

Only Renko said nothing. He slung Jessica's portfolio aside and walked away down the corridor.

Jessica reached the second floor and began to gather up her drawings as she went, clutching them close to her chest. She was panting hard and trying not to cry. As she reached the top of the last flight of stairs, however, she saw Billy Muñóz pick up one of her paintings and hold it up in both hands as if he were going to rip it in half.

'Come and get it!' he taunted her. 'Come and get it before it's too late!'

Jessica took one step, and then another, and then she stumbled. She tried to grab the handrail but her arms were crowded with drawings and she missed. She thought to herself: I'm falling, and she fell.

For one long suspended moment, she looked almost as if she were a talented acrobat, turning a graceful cartwheel on the stairs. She flew through a cloud of paper; she could hear the sheets clapping against each other like applause. One more cartwheel, then another, and she would land in the lobby on her feet, ta-da!, and nobody would ever call her Gimpy ever again.

But her hip caught the metal edge of the stairs, and then her shoulder, and then she was nothing but a tumbling whirl of arms and legs and her head hit the marble-tiled floor at the bottom with a sickening hollow knock.

Class III stood silent for a moment, shocked. Jessica lay

on her side, unmoving. Her limbs all looked as if they were in the wrong position, and her wristwatch was broken. The last of her drawings see-sawed down from the second story and settled beside her.

Fay Perelli knelt down beside Jessica and shook her shoulder.

'Jessica? Jessica? Are you OK? Jessica, say something!'

Jessica's face was gray, and when Fay tried to turn her over a dark pool of blood slid out from under her like a snake and slithered across the tiles toward the door.

'Call a teacher,' Fay whispered. The class stared at her, still in shock.

'Call a teacher!' she shrilled.

Jessica opened her eyes and her room was filled with the strangest light. It was a bright, chilly light, almost blue, the kind of remote radiance you see on a moonlit night. She wondered if she were dead, and this was heaven. She certainly felt as if she were dead. She waited for an angel to come and tell her what to do next. She was still waiting patiently when her eyes closed again.

'Help us.'

Her eyelids flickered.

'Help us, please.' The voice was very close to her ear, and it was high and whispery, like that of a badly frightened five-year-old.

'Mmwhah?' she said. Her lips felt dry and when she tried to lick them they felt all crusty.

'You have to help us, it's coming to take us.'

She turned over and soon she was asleep.

The bright blue light gradually faded to violet and shadows gathered like thickening cobwebs in the corners of her room.

'Help us,' whispered the voice with even greater urgency, but Jessica still slept.

*　　*　　*

Next time she opened her eyes she heard a door closing. Two or three people were discussing something very quietly, just outside her door.

'. . . long way to go yet, but the signs are good . . .'

Hm. That must mean that she would have to walk somewhere, perhaps to another part of heaven, but if the signs were good, she shouldn't have any difficulty in finding her way. Perhaps they were going to send her to be reunited with her parents.

'. . . we've been talking to her, singing her favorite songs – never thought you'd catch me singing "I'm A Loser, Baby, Why Don't You Kill Me?".'

She could feel herself frowning. That sounded so much like Grandpa Willy. But Grandpa Willy wasn't dead, was he? So what was he doing in heaven?

'Once she's fully regained consciousness, she should make very rapid progress – the scan showed no signs of any permanent damage—'

'You have no idea how relieved . . .'

The voices faded. She fell asleep again. The shadow spiders spun their webs thicker and thicker, and soon it was completely dark.

'Help us.'

Jessica stirred and made a whuffling noise.

'Help us.'

She opened her eyes. Suddenly, she was very awake.

'Help us, please. It's coming to get us.'

She sat up and looked around her, but there was nobody there.

'Where are you?' she whispered.

'We're here, we're here. Please, help us. It's coming to get us and it's coming closer.'

'I can't see you,' said Jessica. Her heart was banging, and she was beginning to feel seriously off-balance. She

realized now that this definitely wasn't heaven. This was
her room at Grannie and Grandpa's house: she could even
see her bathrobe hanging on the back of the door. Maybe
she wasn't dead after all, unless heaven was the same as
Earth except that you weren't alive.

'Help us.'

'Where are you? I can't see you.'

'It's coming after us. It's going to take us all.'

'Who's after you?'

There was a faint, quick rustling sound, and then silence.

'Who's after you?' Jessica repeated. 'I can't help you if
I don't know who you are and where you are and why they
want to kill you.'

Again, silence.

Jessica waited and waited but she didn't hear the frightened voice again. She drew back the thick patchwork quilt
on top of her bed and carefully swung her legs around. She
switched on her bedside light, the one with the flower-fairies
on the lampshade. Her right ankle, her good ankle, had
a tight elastic bandage on it, and it was throbbing, as
if she had sprained it. Her left ankle was the same as
always, twisted to one side, with red scars all around it.
She straightened her back and flexed her shoulders. She
felt sore and bruised all over, the way she had felt after
the car crash. She reached up and patted her head. She
found that she was wearing a large turban of bandages,
like the princess in *Ali Baba*. She stood up and limped
over to the mirror; she was shocked by what she saw.
Both of her eyes were surrounded by rainbow-colored
circles and there were big black scabs on her lips. She
was waxy pale and she looked even thinner than she
usually did.

She was still staring at herself when the bedroom door
opened and Grannie came in, all wild white hair and bright
red hand-knitted sweater.

6

'Jessica! Sweetheart! You're awake! Grandpa Willy, will you come quick! Jessica's woken up!'

Grannie put her arm around her and guided her back to her bed. 'How are you feeling, sweetie-pie? Does your head hurt? How about your ankle? Oh my Lord, we've been so worried about you.'

'I'm fine, I think,' Jessica told her. 'I just feel like I fell downstairs or something.'

'That's exactly what happened. You fell downstairs. You dropped your drawings at school and when you tried to pick them up you fell downstairs. You had a terrible concussion.'

Grandpa Willy came in, his hair just as wild and white as Grannie's, and he spread his arms wide to give her a hug. 'I haven't been to bed in five days, fretting about you. Thank God you're OK.'

'Five days? You mean I've been sleeping for five days?'

'That's right. You were in the hospital for two of them, but you were showing all the signs of coming around and the doctor thought it would help you along if we brought you home. You gave yourself one hell of a crack on the bean there.'

Jessica said, 'I don't really remember. I remember I was trying to pick up my drawings but that's all.'

'It'll come back to you, sweetie-pie,' said Grannie, sandwiching Jessica's hand between hers. 'Dr Leeming said that you might suffer a little short-term memory loss. I'm just so glad you're awake.'

'Better get back into bed,' Grandpa Willy suggested. 'Are you hungry at all? Dr Leeming said we could give you some soup when you woke up, if you had the taste for it.'

Jessica shook her head. 'Maybe later. I still feel . . . strange.'

'Of course you do, going to school on Wednesday and waking up the following Monday. Listen, you rest. How

7

about watching TV for a while? I'll bring you up some warm milk.'

'Thanks, Grannie.' Jessica didn't really want any warm milk, but she knew how much pleasure it gave her grandmother to mollycoddle her. In a small way, it helped to ease the pain of losing the girl whose photograph stood on the mantelpiece above the living-room fire. The girl who looked just like Jessica.

'Grannie—' said Jessica, as she went to the door.

'What is it, sweetie-pie?'

'I don't know, maybe I dreamed it. I guess I probably did.'

Her grandmother came back and sat on the side of the bed. 'What is it?' she asked. In the dim light from the beside lamp, her skin was as soft and wrinkled as ruched velvet, and face powder clung to the tiny hairs around her upper lip.

'Is there anybody else living here? Apart from us?'

'I don't understand what you mean.'

'It doesn't matter. It must have been a dream.'

'It wasn't a bad dream, was it?'

'I'm not sure. But there aren't any children staying here, are there?'

'Only you, sweetie-pie.'

She kissed Jessica on the forehead and went downstairs. Jessica sat up in bed, straining her ears. Once she thought she heard another furtive shuffle, and she jumped, but it was only a lump of thawing snow dropping off the roof into the garden below.

The Girl in the Mirror

It was snowing like a thousand burst-open pillows as they crawled out of the city that afternoon. A truck had overturned on the Hutchinson Parkway and they had to take a three-mile detour. Even though it was only three o'clock, the sky was charcoal gray and everybody was driving with snow-clogged headlights.

'We should have left an hour earlier,' said her mother.

'We'll be OK,' said her father. 'Once we get past White Plains, we'll be fine.'

'You know how fussy my mother is about everybody being on time.'

'So why don't you give her a call? Tell her we're just about to hit Danbury.'

'We're miles from Danbury.'

'I know we are. But once we get onto Route six-eighty-four I can really put my foot down.'

In the back of the Buick, on the warm red leather seats, Jessica was playing with two of her fairy figures, Queen Titania and Princess Fay. Oh, Princess Fay, the snow-beasts are flying at us from all sides, what shall we do? Never fear, I shall use my wand to make a wall of glass, and they will never harm us.

'Hello, Mother? It's me. Yes, we're doing fine. We should be passing Danbury in five or ten minutes. Sure. Well, it's snowing here too. I hope you've got some of your hot fruit punch waiting for us!'

'How did she sound?'

'She believed me, if that's what you mean.'

Our magic sleigh will take us through the whirling snow-beasts to the Palace of the Old Ones, where we will be fed with many good things, jellies made from roses and rainwater, peacock pies, swans fashioned out of sugar. There will be music and dancing, and the blowing of many trumpets to salute us.

'Look at this guy, he's weaving all over the road.'

They had caught up with a huge black tractor-trailer with NORTH POLE REFRIGERATED DELIVERY written on the back, and a picture of a penguin with a scarf on, giving them the thumbs-up. Even though it was traveling at less than 20 mph, the truck was swaying from one side of the carriageway to the other and churning up a filthy blizzard of slush and spray, so that her father had to switch his windshield wipers on to full. Jessica liked that, when they flapped really fast, whip whap, whip whap!

Her father flashed his headlights and blew his horn.

'Come on, John, there's no point in getting impatient.'

'All he has to do is pull over and let us pass. Is that too much to ask? Guy's drunk, by the way he's driving.'

More flashing, more horn-blowing. Jessica had the oddest feeling that the penguin was smiling only at her, and giving only her the thumbs-up. Don't worry, kid, you're going to be fine. We shall invite all the penguins and the polar bears to our banquet, Princess Fay, and we shall feed them on mackerel and mint ice-cream.

Her father suddenly put his foot down and swerved the car to the left, starting to overtake.

'John! Don't! You can't see!'

'It's OK, trust me. How well do I know this road? There's a left-hand curve here and if there was anything coming the other way we would have seen it.'

They drew up alongside the tractor-trailer and Jessica's

window was filled with its huge sizzling wheels. Her father accelerated faster and faster but the truck seemed to go on forever; it felt as if they would take a week to get past it.

'He's putting his foot down! What's the matter with him? Can't he see me?'

The windshield wipers flapped and flapped but there was so much spray coming from the truck's wheels that her father was practically driving blind.

'John!' said her mother. 'John, pull back, let him go!'

'No way, not this bastard.' They edged forward little by little until they were neck-and-neck with the truck, and suddenly they were clear of the spray. That was when the interior of the Buick was abruptly flooded with brilliant light. Jessica heard her mother say, 'Oh, God,' very quietly, as if she were talking only to herself.

The oncoming panel-van hit them head-on. Jessica could never remember hearing any noise, although there must have been. But she remembered the jolt of her seat-belt across her chest and her fairies flying through the car, and then a terrible bumpety-bumpety-bumpety as they careered down a steep graveled embankment and into a stand of pine trees. There was a bang that almost knocked her teeth out, but she didn't feel any pain, even though her mother's seat had been forced backward and downward by the impact and comprehensively crushed her foot.

She remembered the car door being opened, and a flash-light shining in her eyes. 'Everybody OK?'

'Call nine-one-one, Lance. Looks like these two have bought the farm.'

'How about you, little lady? Are you OK?'

'I've lost my fairies.'

'OK, don't you worry, we'll find your fairies. Let's see if we can get you out of there.'

She stood by the bedroom window, looking out over the

snowy garden. This morning Dr Leeming had called to examine her and had taken her turban off. Her hair had been shaved off in a triangular patch and there were seven stitches in her scalp. She still had to wear a dressing, but now she could cover her head with a red-and-yellow silk scarf that used to belong to her mother.

In the center of the garden stood a bronze statuette of Pan, with cloven hoofs, and horns, and a sly, untrustworthy smile. He was dancing and playing his pipes, even though there was a large blob of snow on top of his head.

She looked around her room. It was hard to believe that it was nearly eleven months since the car crash. Her room on East 86th Street had been airy and pale and very modern, even though the basketwork armchairs had been overpopulated with all of her various fairies and elves, and her painting-table had been cluttered with pencils, brushes, pots of water and squeezed-out tubes of paint.

Grandpa Willy had lived in this house since 1948, and even then it was already eighty-five years old. It stood about two miles out of New Milford, on the road to Allen's Corners, in six and a half acres of its own grounds. It had steeply sloping roofs and very tall brick chimneys and Jessica could never imagine why anybody would have wanted to build it, unless they had been wealthy and lonely and sad. Like every other bedroom, her own room was wallpapered with pasture roses and wild irises and blessed thistles. The wallpaper was faded now, and stained in places, but she supposed that Grannie and Grandpa Willy didn't notice things like that any more. Grandpa Willy had walked in this morning with dried egg yolk on his vest, and Grannie was always wearing odd socks.

On one side of the room loomed the large closet in which she kept all of her clothes. It was so tall that it almost reached to the ceiling, and it was veneered in walnut, which had knots that looked like eyes and dark jagged shapes that looked like animals' faces. On the other side, next to the brown-tiled fireplace, stood her dressing-table, which also had her computer on it and her carved-wood mirror. She talked to the girl in the mirror every day. The girl in the mirror didn't have any friends, either – even though, exactly like Jessica, she was skinny-waisted and pretty, with glossy brown shoulder-length hair and large dark eyes and a slightly elfin look. Grannie's mother had come from Norway, that's what Grannie said, and that's why Jessica looked like that. There were lots of elves in Norway, and they often married humans.

She decided to go downstairs. It was all very well being the fairy princess in the attic, but she was growing bored now, and hungry. She could smell ham boiling and cookies baking. Grannie may have fussed too much, but she was a wonderful cook.

'Help us.'

She was reaching for her bathrobe, but she stopped, with her hand still raised. A cold feeling slowly crept down her back like a melting snowball.

'Help us,' the voice repeated. It sounded weaker than it had before, but it was just as frightened. 'It's coming closer. You have to help us.'

'I can't—' Jessica began, but then she had to clear her throat. 'I can't see you. How can I help you if I don't know who you are?'

'Help us, there's a way.'

'What way? I don't understand. I can't even see you – what can I do?'

'You don't know what it's going to do to us. It's going to take us all, but it's going to do far worse than that.'

'Where are you? Let me see you!'

'We're here. We're here. Help us.'

The voice seemed to come from somewhere very close, only inches away from her ear, and yet it seemed to be all around her, too, like fifty people all whispering at once.

She looked toward the fireplace. The voice must be coming from there, that was why it echoed so much. Somebody was whispering into the fireplace in another room, and the sound carried through all the complicated chimneys until it came out here. Whether her grandmother knew it or not, there must be other children living in the house somewhere. Maybe they had run away from home. Or perhaps they were orphans, who had escaped from a local orphanage.

Whoever they were, Jessica decided that she had to find them. Whatever was after them, they were scared for their lives.

'Tell me where you are,' she said, clearly. 'Don't be frightened. Tell me what room you're in, and I'll come and rescue you.'

'We're here. Help us.'

Jessica was about to ask the voice again when Grannie appeared, wearing an apron and a big, hot smile. 'I thought I heard you calling, sweetie-pie. Do you want to come downstairs? There's chocolate muffins and pecan cookies and some of my lemon cake, if you're interested.'

Jessica thought she heard a furtive scamper, like a rat running behind the skirting-board. 'Yes please,' she said. 'I'd like that.'

'Is everything all right? You look . . . worried about something.'

'I'm fine. My head doesn't hurt nearly so much. I think I might do some drawing this afternoon.'

She was following Grannie down the wide oak staircase when the front doorbell rang. Grandpa Willy came across the hallway with his paper under his arm and said, 'Don't worry, I'll get it!'

He opened the large oak door. Inside the house it was

winter-gloomy, but outside the light from the snow was dazzling. At first, blinking, Jessica didn't recognize the boy standing in the porch. He was pale and skinny with a blond crewcut and his nose was red from the cold.

'Young man called Renko here to see you,' said Grandpa Willy.

Where Are the Children?

They sat at the big scrubbed-pine kitchen table and Grannie brought them muffins, cookies and fruit bread. The kitchen was always warm in winter because Grannie cooked on a massive old cast-iron range. On the walls there were glossy green tiles with convolvulus patterns on them, and the floor was covered in green-and-cream linoleum squares, which were always so shiny you could slide across them in your socks.

On either side of the range there were two small stained-glass windows, with apple trees and puffy clouds and faraway hills. When she was little, Jessica had always wondered what it would be like to live in Stained-Glass Window Land, and walk along the winding path between the apple trees, to see what lay beyond.

Renko had taken off his huge gray windbreaker with the fake-fur collar and Grandpa Willy had hung it up for him. He looked skinnier than ever in his blue-and-white Connecticut Huskies sweatshirt, and his wrists were so thin that his bracelet watch was loose. He sat opposite Jessica, but kept his eyes fixed on his chocolate muffin.

'Milk or Seven-Up?' asked Grannie.

'Oh, Seven-Up's great, thank you.'

'Are you in Jessica's class? What did you say your name was, Ringo?'

'Renko, ma'am. David Renko, but everybody calls me

just Renko. Yes . . . Jessica and me, we're both in Mrs Walker's class.'

'Well, it was very thoughtful of you to pay her a visit.'

Renko quickly glanced up at Jessica, and she saw for the first time how gray his eyes were. Gray like pigeon feathers.

From the top of the stairs, Grandpa Willy called out, 'Where d'you put my clean red flannels, Mildred? I can't find the dang things anywhere.'

Grannie said, 'Excuse me a moment. Your grandpa, honestly. He couldn't find his flannels if he was wearing them.'

She went out of the kitchen and Jessica and Renko were left alone. Neither of them touched their muffin. Neither of them spoke, not for almost half a minute. Then Jessica said 'Why—?' and Renko said 'How—?' both at the same time, and then both of them stopped and stared at each other.

'You first,' said Jessica.

Renko cleared his throat. 'I was going to ask you – you know, if you were OK.'

'I'm OK. I was going to ask you why you came to see me.'

Renko lowered his eyes again. 'I guess I came to say sorry.'

'Sorry? Why?'

'What happened to you, that was totally my fault. Totally.'

'I don't really remember much about it, to tell you the truth. I know that I was picking up my drawings, and I fell downstairs, but that's about all.'

Renko said, 'It was me. Me and Sue-Anne and the rest of the gang, we were all teasing you. No we weren't, we were bullying you. I dropped all of your pictures down the staircase. It was a totally dorkish thing to do, wasn't it? But

17

I was showing off in front of the others. Like I said, I'm really sorry.'

'OK . . .' said Jessica. 'I didn't even realize it was you.'

'I was a total dork, that's all.'

Jessica looked at him for a while, and then she said, 'I'm getting much better now, anyhow. They're taking my stitches out Tuesday. Look – why don't you eat your muffin, they're really good.'

Renko took a bite of muffin, and began to chew it. 'I feel like such an idiot,' he said. 'It was just that Sue-Anne and the others . . . well, I don't know. Sue-Anne's a really nice person when you get to know her, but she always has to be the center of attention. Otherwise, you know, she's the Incredible Sulk.'

'I never tried to be the center of attention.'

'You didn't have to try, did you? You came to school last winter and your parents were dead and you had this walking-stick. So you were, like, somebody out of a story. As well as being pretty.'

'I'm not pretty. What are you talking about?'

'You don't think you're pretty?' Renko seemed incredulous. 'How can you say that?'

'Sue-Anne's pretty. Fay Perelli, she's pretty.'

'Sure they are, but they're like sort of, I don't know, cheerleader pretty. You're not like that.' He swallowed. 'You're like, *strange* pretty.'

'Is that why everybody's been so horrible to me?'

Renko didn't look up. 'I guess you didn't really fit in, either. I mean the fact your parents were dead and all those fairies you drew, and all those poems you wrote about fairies. And the teachers were all really nice to you, too, and I guess that made some people jealous. Not me, but some of the girls, for sure. Sue-Anne, Charlene, one or two others.' He took a breath, and then he said, 'We've been giving you a real hard time and I'm totally sorry. That's all I came to say. I think I'd better go now.'

'No, don't. You haven't had any cookies yet.'

'Really, I should go.'

Jessica said, 'Do you want to be friends?'

Renko hesitated. 'Sure,' he said, although it was more of a question than an answer.

'Have some cookies, then,' she insisted, and passed over the plate. Renko took one and bit into it. It crumbled so much that he had to push it all into his mouth at once.

Jessica glanced toward the door to make sure that her grandmother was still out of earshot, and then she leaned across the table and whispered, 'There are some children trapped in this house.'

'Woff?' asked Renko, spraying crumbs.

'I've heard them. I don't know how many. Sometimes it sounds like only one, but other times it sounds like dozens and dozens. I think they're locked in a room somewhere but they're calling for help up the chimney, so that I can hear them out of my fireplace.'

'You're kidding me! Have you told your grandparents?'

Jessica shook her head. 'How can I? Supposing it's them that's locked them up!'

'What do you mean? They're your *grandparents*! I mean, I don't like to be rude but talk about a couple of old coots! What would they want to lock up a whole bunch of kids for?'

'I don't know, but they keep saying, "Help us, help us, it's coming after us." Like they're really, really scared.'

'You're sure you heard them? You don't think maybe that knock on the nut—'

Jessica shook her head emphatically. 'The first time I heard them was when I was coming out of my concussion. Actually I thought I was dead, but when I knew I wasn't dead I thought I must be dreaming, or hearing things. But

I heard them again this morning, just before you arrived, when I was wide awake, so I can't have been hearing things. They're real, and they're trapped in this house somewhere.'

'So what are you going to do? Call the cops?'

'No. I want to find out what's going on first. I mean, Grannie and Grandpa Willy would never do anything wrong, at least I don't think so, and what would I do if they were arrested? Where would I go?'

'You need to search the place,' said Renko.

'I know. It's just that it's kind of scary, doing it on your own.'

Renko took another cookie and snapped it in half. 'I hope you're not suggesting what I think you're suggesting.'

Jessica nodded.

'Hey, I don't know. I'm supposed to be going to basket-ball practice at eleven o'clock.'

'We've got plenty of time. Please.'

At that moment, Grannie came back into the kitchen. 'You young people have hardly eaten a thing! Something wrong with my chocolate muffins? They're not poison, you know!'

'Oh no, they're outstanding, thanks,' said Renko. 'I had a big breakfast, is all.'

'I'll pack you some to take home. And how about some cookies too?'

'Sure, that'd be great.'

'I'm just going to show Renko my room,' said Jessica.

'That's fine,' smiled Grannie. 'I hope Renko likes fairies.'

'Actually I was going to let him take a look at my CD collection.'

'Fairies are extremely cool, too,' said Renko, with a completely serious expression on his face. 'Fairies are extremely cool, too!' Jessica giggled, as they ran up the wide oak staircase. 'What made you say that?'

'I don't know. But if you like them so much, maybe they are. You know, maybe I'm, like, missing something.'

They went into her bedroom. The low winter sun was shining directly into the window and everything was blessed with a gold-and-amber glow. Renko looked around at all the fairy dolls and the elves and the drawings that Jessica had pinned up on the wall – fairies flying through clouds of thistle-down; elves playing musical instruments made of acorns and horse-chestnuts and river reeds; fairies in crystal coaches drawn by stag beetles.

Jessica sat on the bed and watched him. When he had finished, he turned and looked at her and there was an unspoken question in his eyes.

'I suppose you think I'm much too old for stuff like this.'

He shrugged. 'If you like it, it's cool. My mom collects teddy bears.'

'I always liked fairies, ever since I was very little. I liked them because they were so tiny and pretty and they lived in a land where everybody was always happy. I had a younger sister called Eileen who died when I was six and I suppose that was something to do with it. My mom and dad were never really happy after that. They always said they were happy, but it was like being at the seaside, you know, when the sun goes behind a cloud and never comes out again.'

'And then your folks got killed.'

'Yes,' she said.

He went to the window and looked out. The sun made his crewcut shine like fairy thistle. 'I really dig that dude in the middle of the garden.'

'That statue? That's Pan. He was the Greek god of nature. Whenever he appeared, he frightened travelers so much that they ran for their lives. That's where the word "panic" comes from.'

'Hey . . . you learn something new every day.'

'Well, Grannie told me that.'

'Pretty cool granny, to have a scary dude like that in her garden. My granny has this kind of illuminated waterfall thing. It looks like something out of Las Vegas. My grandpa hates it because it makes this trickling noise and he keeps having to get up and go to the bathroom.'

Jessica smiled. There was silence between them for a while, and then they heard a door close and the sound of Grandpa Willy creaking his way down the staircase.

'Come on,' said Jessica, 'we can search for the children now.'

'Do you really think we should? I mean, supposing your grandparents catch us at it?'

'They won't. Grandpa Willy's gone down for his muffins and coffee and he won't come back up again for ages.'

Renko blew out his cheeks. 'OK, then. If you say so. But if we get caught, don't say I didn't warn you.'

They tiptoed out on to the landing. They could hear Grannie and Grandpa Willy talking in the kitchen. They seemed to be arguing about something, although Jessica couldn't make out what they were saying, except when Grandpa Willy suddenly snapped, 'You're the most stubborn woman I ever met in my life! I've seen whole teams of mules more reasonable than you!'

Jessica and Renko looked at each other and pulled faces. 'Maybe one of them wants to keep the children locked up and the other doesn't,' Jessica suggested.

'Ssh,' said Renko.

They crept along the landing to the bedroom door next to Jessica's. It was locked, but the key was in it. Jessica pressed her ear to the dark oak paneling and listened.

'Hear anything?' asked Renko.

'No. I'll try knocking.'

She rapped softly on the door and said, 'Hello? Hello? Is there anybody in there?'

They waited, but nobody answered. 'Let's just take a look for ourselves,' said Renko.

'Be careful. If there's any children inside, we don't want them rushing out and making a noise.'

'OK, I'll be careful.'

Renko slowly turned the key; the landing was so quiet that they could hear the lock-levers clicking. Grannie and Grandpa Willy seemed to have stopped arguing for a while, and all they could hear from downstairs was the clinking of china. 'What if—' Jessica began, but Renko pressed his finger to his lips and eased the door open. It gave a low, uneasy groan, but he pushed it wider and wider until they could see into the room.

It was an empty bedroom, a little smaller than Jessica's but decorated in much the same way, with flowery wallpaper and drapes. The bed was covered with a pink candlewick bedspread, on which an ancient doll was propped. Her curly hair was half unglued from her scalp and her eyes had dropped out, so that she had only vacant sockets. Renko went over and picked her up and she let out a ghastly, throat-cancerous 'Mam . . . ma!'

'Well . . . no children in here. You can't sort of think where their voices might have been actually, like, coming from? I mean, except from out of the fireplace? I wouldn't like to think they were stuck up the chimney.'

Jessica said, 'No. Let's try the big bedroom over there.'

Renko took a last look around the room and followed Jessica to the door.

It was then that the voices whispered, 'Help us.'

'What?'

Jessica took hold of his arm. 'Listen! That was them!'

'I thought it was you.'

'No – listen, it's them!'

They stood silent and still for nearly a minute. 'I don't hear anything,' said Renko at last. 'I mean, maybe it's just

the wind blowing across the stack. That happens sometimes. It's like when you blow across the top of an empty
Coke bottle.'

'Help us. It's coming closer.'

Renko stared at Jessica and his mouth opened and closed.

'You heard that?' said Jessica.

'You bet I did. Holy Moly. That wasn't any wind.'

Up in the Attic

They crossed the landing, treading as lightly as they could because the floorboards groaned. Renko tried the handle of the big bedroom door, but it was locked, and there was no key in it. He bent down on one knee and peered through the keyhole.

'What can you see?'

'Nothing. A curtain. Part of a window.'

Jessica tapped on the door panel with her knuckle and called out, 'Hello? Hello? Is there anybody there?'

They waited, but there was no reply. She tapped again, and hissed, 'Don't be afraid! We're here to help you!'

There was still no answer. Eventually Renko stood up and said, 'There's nobody in there, Jessica. We'll have to look through all of the other rooms.'

Together they went along the upstairs corridor, trying every door handle and tapping at every door they couldn't open. The house had nine bedrooms altogether, as well as a box room and Grannie's sewing-room, but the bedrooms they could open were empty, and there was no reply from the rooms that were locked.

'Forget it,' said Renko. 'There's nobody here.'

'But you heard them.'

'I know I heard them. I'm not saying I didn't.'

'So where are they, then?'

'Maybe they're in the attic.'

'They sounded so close.'

'Yeah, well, it's amazing how voices can travel along chimneys and drainpipes and stuff.'

'All right then. Let's take a look in the attic.'

She was about to open the narrow cream-painted door that led up to the attic when Grandpa Willy came puffing up the stairs. 'How's it going, kids?'

'Fine, thanks, Grandpa. I was just showing Renko my CDs.'

'You like that stuff, Renko?'

'Beck, and Eminem? Sure.'

'Andy Williams is more my style. "The Days of Wine and Roses". Jeez, I think I ate two muffins too many. I think I need to lie down.'

Jessica glanced at Renko and she could tell he was thinking the same thing. They couldn't explore the attic while Grandpa Willy was up here.

'Renko was just leaving, Grandpa.'

'OK then. Good to meet you, Renko. Good to see some of Jessica's friends paying her a visit for a change. You come again.'

'Yes, sir. I certainly will, sir.'

Grandpa Willy went off to his bedroom in a fit of coughing while Jessica and Renko went downstairs. Renko took his coat off the rack and shuffled himself into it.

'Grannie and Grandpa are going out tomorrow afternoon. They always go out Thursdays for their over-sixties' club. Do you want to come round?'

'I don't know . . . I'm kind of busy tomorrow.'

'How about Saturday? Do you want to come around Saturday? I could make pizza or something. I make really good pizza.'

'I don't know. I'll have to see what I'm doing.'

'I'm going to take a look in the attic even if you don't come with me.'

Renko hesitated for a moment, and then he said, 'Listen . . .

I don't know if I really want to get involved in this. I heard something, for sure. I heard somebody talking, I'm not saying that I didn't. But, you know, maybe it's just one of those what-d'you-call-its. Natural phenomena. Like when you can see cities that are hundreds of miles away, floating in the sky. Only this is voices.'

'So you're not going to come, then?'

Renko gave a non-committal shrug.

'That's all right,' said Jessica. 'At least you came around to say you were sorry, even if I didn't know what it was you were supposed to be sorry about.'

'Yeah. Sorry.'

She opened the door for him and he stepped out into the wintry chill. She watched him walk all the way down the pathway to the gate, but he didn't turn round once. The sky was orange and the first few flakes of fresh snow were falling.

'Jessica! Is that front door open? There's a howling draft in here!'

Jessica closed the door and the log fire in the hallway billowed out a cloud of eye-stinging smoke. She went into the kitchen where Grannie was making pies. 'Sorry, Grannie. I was just saying goodbye.'

'That Ringo's a nice boy,' said Grannie, sifting flour onto her pastry board. 'You should ask him around more often.'

Jessica said nothing, but sat down at the kitchen table and started to draw patterns in the flour. This is the secret sign that shows you the way to the fairy kingdom. A circle, and a knot, and a pattern of evening stars. Whenever you see this sign, you will know that the Fairy Kingdom is closer than you think. But whether you've got the courage to go there, that's a different matter altogether.

'Jessica, will you stop messing around with my flour, girl!'

Jessica brushed away the secret sign, and then clapped

her hands together to get rid of the flour. Clap your hands once and the fairies will hear you. Clap them twice and the door will open. Clap them three times and you will always get more than you bargained for.

She went back up to her bedroom and stood at the window. The snow was hurrying down all over the garden, so thick that she could barely see the statue of Pan. 'Strange pretty', Renko had called her. She pressed her forehead against the window-pane so that she could feel the cold in her brain. For the first time in a long time, she felt desperately lonely.

Jessica lay in bed and listened to Grannie and Grandpa Willy go through their usual pantomime performance of going to bed.

'Did you lock the back door, Willy?'

'No, Mildred, I left it wide open with a sign saying, "Come on in, burglars, and help yourselves!"'

'Have you washed your teeth yet, Willy?'

'I would if I could find the dang things.'

They opened and closed the bathroom door about twenty-eight times, and flushed the toilet over and over, as if a flush-toilet was a novelty. They had an argument in the corridor about who was getting in whose way, and then they closed their bedroom door, still arguing, and then they opened it again to switch off the landing light.

'You never remember to switch off that light!'

'Well, why didn't you tell me it was on?'

'Why should I tell you? You're not blind!'

'No, but the way you nag, I'm practically deaf!'

Eventually there was nothing but the feather-soft pattering of snow against the window, and the eerie light of a late-November night. Jessica waited for nearly half an hour, and then she climbed out of bed and put on her bathrobe. In the top drawer of her dressing-table, under her neatly folded panties, was Grandpa's big red flashlight, which she had borrowed from the closet in the kitchen.

She carefully opened her bedroom door, and listened. The landing was almost totally dark, except for the faintest reflected light from the hallway downstairs. At this time of the evening, the house was talking to itself about the day gone by. The ashy logs in the living-room fireplace suddenly lurched and dropped. The range in the kitchen started a slow, regular ticking as the hob cooled down. The clocks chimed; the plumbing rattled as the tanks in the attic filled up. And on winter nights like this, with so many pounds of snow on top of the roof, the whole house would creak and complain, an arthritic old man in a heavy overcoat.

At the far end of the landing stood a tall bureau and on top of the bureau was a vase with ostrich feathers in it, with an oval mirror behind it. In the darkness, the vase looked like the head of a giant vulture, with a scrawny neck and a hooked beak. Jessica stared at it before she opened the attic door, just to make sure that it wasn't a vulture, but even when she stared she didn't feel sure.

Jessica crossed the landing to the attic door. She lifted the latch, opened the door and shone the flashlight up the narrow wooden stairs. She could smell dust, and something else, like faded pot-pourri. There was a light switch there, but she didn't want to turn it on in case Grandpa Willy made one of his regular visits to the bathroom and saw it shining under the door.

She climbed the stairs as quietly as she could. If there were any children up here, she didn't want to wake them. She reached the top, where there was a banister, and shone the flashlight quickly from one end of the attic to the other.

All she could see were steamer trunks, boxes, old-fashioned lamp standards, heaps and heaps of books and magazines, a treadle sewing-machine and two dismantled brass beds. In the darker recesses of the attic, however, she could make out other shapes: something that looked like a black dog, lying on its side; and something that looked like a man, bent over it. And something that looked like a huge spider, dangling from the ceiling: something which idly swayed.

'Hello?' she whispered. She paused, and then repeated, 'Hello?' but much more loudly.

She took a step forward, and then another, and then she trod on something that felt pleated and sickeningly soft. It let out a hideous wheezing noise, and she stumbled back against the banister, her heart banging and pins-and-needles prickling all the way down her back. She shone the flashlight toward the floor, and there was a broken piano-accordion, leaking out its last cacophonous breath.

'Scaredy-cat,' she chided herself. But all the same she made her way into the further reaches of the attic with much greater caution, sweeping the flashlight from side to side to make sure that she didn't tread on anything else.

She couldn't see any children here, but there were heaps of gray blankets at the other end, under the sloping eaves, and she thought she ought to look underneath them, just to make sure. That would mean making her way between the black dog and the man who was leaning over it.

It couldn't possibly be a black dog, not really; and it couldn't be a man; and as she came nearer she expected the shapes to resolve themselves into what they really were. A black blanket, maybe, and a coat hung over a chair. Yet she was only six metres away from them now and they still looked like a dog and a man. She shone the flashlight directly at the back of the man's head and she was sure she could see the curve of his ear, his dusty gray hair.

She stopped. She was too frightened to carry on. The man hadn't moved, and neither had the dog, but she was less than five metres away from them now and they hadn't changed.

She could even see the dog's red tongue, and its gleaming white incisors.

'Ah – pardon me,' she said, in a voice so high that it didn't sound like her own.

The man didn't move, and neither did the dog.

'I'm looking for some children.'

Still the man didn't move. Jessica kept his head in the wavering beam of Grandpa's flashlight. She didn't know if she ought to retreat downstairs or take another few steps forward.

'Hello?' she said. 'I'm looking for some children!'

She heard her breath squeak with anxiety as she took one more step toward the man, and then another. Please don't be a real man, please be a coat. She took another step, and then another. She reached out to touch his shoulder.

And then the man whipped his head around and for one split-second she saw a dark face like the face of a devil and wild white eyes without any pupils and then the desk-lamp fell from the chair with a clatter and the rug that was wrapped around it fell too.

For a moment she couldn't move. But then, with her heart palpitating, she shone the flashlight onto the floor. The devil's face was nothing but a brown glass Tiffany lampshade, with diamond-shaped patterns of clear glass all around it. His hair was nothing but the fringe around the rug. And when she directed the flashlight toward the black dog, she saw that it was only a golfing-bag, with the front pocket unzipped to reveal its red leather lining and two or three white plastic tees.

She turned around. The spider-thing that had been swaying on the ceiling was a beaded lampshade, stirring in the draft that blew under the eaves.

She was still trembling, but she had never felt so relieved in her life. She felt that she had suddenly grown up, and realized for the first time that the frightening shapes she saw in the darkness were only imaginary. The bathrobe hanging on the back of her bedroom door never turned into an evil goblin, even at midnight, and the hunched creature who sat in the corner was only her jeans, thrown over the back of her chair.

Stepping over the golfing-bag, she made her way toward the heaps of gray blankets. The roof was so low here that she had to bend double. The blankets were spread all the way across the width of the roof, and they were covering a series of lumps and bumps. Now that she had seen the man and the dog for what they were, she knew that there couldn't be children under here, but all the same she felt that she had to look.

She knelt down beside the edge of the blankets, and lifted one up. It was very difficult to see what was under it. She saw what looked like a brown velvet sleeve, and a small black lace-up boot, very worn-out.

She dragged the blanket back further. The blanket dust tickled her throat and prickled her eyes. There was a velvet suit there, only a small one, a child's size, and a jumble of other clothes, socks and rolled-up nightshirts and tweed knickerbockers. Then she saw something oval and pale.

The blankets were heaped one on top of the other, so they were difficult to lift. But in the end she manged to pull back one layer, and then another. She crawled forward, over the clothes, and then she saw what the pale thing was.

It was a child's face, with its eyes closed as if it were sleeping, or dead.

Chairs and Clothes

S he jumped back in shock, hitting her shoulder against the eaves. But the child was lying there quite serenely, and didn't stir. It was covered with a navy-blue winter overcoat, with two empty gloves dangling from the sleeves on tapes. Jessica's mother used to do that when she was little, so that she wouldn't lose them. She leaned closer, but she couldn't tell if the child was a boy or a girl.

She didn't know what to do. She couldn't think why Grannie and Grandpa Willy would want to imprison a child up here in the attic – but what would they do to her if she told them that she had found it? She tried to hear if the child was breathing, but the cold-water tank was still filling up, and the gurgling of water drowned out everything. If the child was alive, how did it manage to sleep under all those blankets without suffocating? If it was dead, on the other hand, why wasn't it rotting? Its skin was sallow but it was absolutely flawless, like an angel.

Jessica knelt beside the child and hesitantly held out her hand. Should she wake it up? After all, it had been calling for help, hadn't it? But supposing it was dead?

Summoning all her courage, she tugged back the blankets a little further. She caught her breath. There was another child, sleeping close by. A girl, no more than four, half buried under another coat.

Gasping with effort, Jessica dragged all the blankets away, and it was then that she discovered three more children, all with their eyes closed. When she saw the last child, she cried out, 'Ah!' in fright, but then she immediately understood what the children were, and she almost laughed with relief. The last child had no coat spread over him, and he was nothing but a face with no body.

She crawled toward him on her hands and knees. He looked as if he was almost the same age as she was, sixteen and a half. He had a broad forehead and a long narrow nose and he seemed to be very sad. But he was only an empty mask, molded out of wax.

Jessica lifted the overcoats that appeared to be covering the other children, and they were the same. Five masks, not sleeping, not dead, but simply a poignant memento of five little brothers and sisters who were probably old men and women by now, if any of them were still alive.

She looked at them. Even now that she knew what they were, they were so realistic that she almost expected them to open their eyes and stare at her.

'Who are you?' she asked. 'Who left you up here in the attic?'

She touched each of them on the forehead, very lightly, almost like a benediction, and then she pulled back the blankets and covered them up again.

Halfway through the night, the snow stopped and the house fell silent. Jessica couldn't sleep, even when her bedside clock flicked on to 3:45 A.M. She kept thinking about the children's faces in the attic, and imagined that she could hear them whispering to each other under their blankets.

She might have slept for a while; she wasn't sure. She thought she could hear her mother coming into the room and moving around, picking up her clothes and tidying her dressing-table. You didn't die, Mommy, after all. Where have you been all this time? I've been waiting for you here at Grannie and Grandpa Willy's and I've been waiting so long.

Her eyes filled with tears. Her mother bent over her, stroked her hair and shushed her. Mommy, I waited and waited for you and you never came. Why did they say you were dead? But her mother kept on stroking her hair and saying, 'Shush . . . shush . . .' even though Jessica didn't want to go back to sleep.

'Shush . . . shush . . . help ush . . . shush . . . help us . . . shush . . . help us, please! Help us!'

Jessica sat up with a jolt. As she did so, she felt something flurry in her hair, and there was a flicker on the wallpaper next to her, like a flower unfolding in a speeded-up film. She struggled frantically out of bed and stumbled over to the other side of the room. Her sleep-T was clinging to her and her forehead was crowned with perspiration. She stared at the wallpaper, panting, but it didn't appear to have changed. The same faded pasture roses, the same slender stems. Yet she was certain that she had felt fingers trailing through her hair, and that when she had woken up the wallpaper pattern had hurriedly rearranged itself.

Cautiously, she returned to her bed and switched on her bedside lamp. The roses on the wallpaper had always put her in mind of children's faces, and their stems had always looked like little arms and legs. The irises looked like thin, austere nuns, while the blessed thistles were fierce little soldiers. But she had only imagined that she had seen something, hadn't she, in the same way that she had imagined the man and the black dog in the attic?

She climbed back beneath the covers, but she kept the light on and she stayed as far away from the wall as she could. She stared at the wallpaper for almost half an hour, but it didn't move, and nobody touched her hair, and nobody whispered. Just before five o'clock, her eyelids drooped and she fell asleep.

She was woken at nine the next morning by the sound

of vacuum cleaning. She sat up in bed and switched off her bedside light. It was a dazzling sunny day, and the snow on the roof was dripping. She took a long look at the wallpaper. She even reached out and touched it. But it was only wallpaper, with roses and irises and blessed thistles, not children or nuns or soldiers.

She dressed in a three-quarter-length blue velvet dress with a lacy collar. It made her look very old-fashioned, but she loved dresses like that, especially with big lace-up boots.

'Morning, Lazybones,' smiled Grannie when she came into the kitchen. 'What do you want for your breakfast?'

'Just Cheerios, thanks, Grannie.'

Grace, the cleaner, was polishing the brass rail that ran along the front of the range. 'How are you, Jessica? Your granny told me all about your accident.'

'I'm OK, thanks, Grace. My head's still a bit sore, but I can go back to school next week, once they take out the stitches.'

'I had stitches once,' Epiphany boasted. Epiphany was Grace's only daughter, thirteen years old. She was sitting at the kitchen table threading plastic beads. Epiphany had strikingly large eyes, which looked even bigger because she wore magnifying spectacles. Her hair was braided into cornrows, and there were big golden hoops in her ears. Today she was wearing a pink Benetton sweatshirt and jeans, and bright red Kickers.

Jessica sat down beside her. 'When did you ever have stitches, Piff?'

'I was nine. I was extra good for a whole week and I helped with washing the dishes and making the beds and everything and I never gave my momma no lip, so that I was a perfect angel.'

'So what happened?'

'I thought that if I was a perfect angel I could fly, so I jumped off the carport roof and fell head-first into a wheelbarrow and cut my mouth here, look.' She pulled down her bottom lip to reveal a faint white scar.

'If you want to be an angel it takes more than just a week of being good,' said Jessica. 'You have to be good for your whole entire life.'

'Well, I know that now, don't I? But let me tell you something – trying to be good for a whole week, that sure felt like my whole entire life.'

'What are you making?'

'These are voodoo bracelets like the ones that women wear in Gabon. They give women power over men and dogs. Well, same thing, really.'

Grannie came over with a bowl and a jug of cold milk and a packet of Cheerios. 'You'll change your mind, child, when you get older.'

'No I won't, ever. Men think they rule the world but women are ten hundred times smarter. All men care about is baseball, beer and self-gratification.'

Grace looked at her daughter and then at Grannie, smiled, and gave a little shake of her head. Grace's father had walked out on the family two and a half years ago, and ever since then Epiphany had been a fanatical little-league feminist. Her doctor had said not to worry: it was only a way of handling her pain.

Jessica poured out her cereal and began to eat. 'What are you doing today, Piff?'

'Don't know . . . nothing much. Me and some friends might go skating if Millard's Pond is still frozen over. Or maybe I'll stay at home and I'll finish off these magic bracelets.'

Jessica picked one up. It was made up of ten or eleven strands of red and black beads, all twisted together to make a spiral.

'If you wear that one, your man has to cook your dinner for you.'

Jessica picked up another, green and yellow. 'So what does this do?'

'That one's for making your man wash your feet by licking them.'

'Yuck, I wouldn't want a man licking my feet!' She munched cereal for a while and then said, 'Do you really believe in magic?'

'Of course I do.'

'I mean, do you believe in other lands that people can't usually see?'

Epiphany stopped threading beads and frowned at her solemnly. 'What kind of other lands you talking about?'

'Like – I don't know, like Fairyland.'

Epiphany wrinkled up her nose. 'Fairyland? Are you serious?'

'I don't exactly mean Fairyland . . . I mean somewhere different, but really close. Like a whole world, except that we can't see it, only little bits of it, now and again, especially when we aren't expecting it. I mean, did you ever see something and it looked like something else?'

Epiphany thought about that for a moment, and then she nodded. 'I saw an owl once, a baby owl. It fell off a branch in the back of our yard.'

'What did you do?'

'I put a washbowl over it so that the cats wouldn't get it, and then I told my momma. My momma called the vet, but when he lifted up the washbowl there was nothing underneath it but a dried-up old bath sponge. Same sponge I threw out the bathroom window the summer before.'

Grace laughed and said, 'She wasn't wearing her glasses, that was the trouble.'

But Jessica looked at Epiphany intently and said, 'I'm talking about something else. I'm talking about things you see out of the corner of your eye, but when you look at them straight on they're not there. I'm talking about things you see in the dark, but when you switch the light on they've gone back to being chairs or clothes.'

Epiphany carried on stringing her beads. Jessica watched her, thinking she wasn't going to answer, but after a while she said, 'I've seen something like that.'

'What was it?'

'There was a shadow on my bedroom wall once. It looked just like a hunched-up man. I knew it couldn't be a hunched-up man because my mom was downstairs talking to my Aunt Ellie. My bedroom door was open a little ways and it was only the shadow from the plant that stands in the hallway. But I couldn't stop staring at it and I couldn't help myself from feeling scared because it still looked like a hunched-up man.'

'Is that all?'

'No,' said Epiphany, shaking her head so emphatically that the hoops in her ears jingled. 'I heard my momma coming along the corridor and I thought, Oh no, the hunched-up man is going to get her! But before I could do anything the shadow ran all the way across my bedroom wall and disappeared into the corner. And it wasn't a plant. It was a hunched-up man, or maybe some kind of a monster.'

'That's true?'

'Cross my heart and spit in my eye.'

'So where do you think it went?'

'I don't know. It just slipped into the corner, like – like there was a way through.'

'A way through to where?'

'To where you're talking about . . . another world.'

Grannie had been drying up cups. 'Are you finished with your breakfast yet, Jessica? Grace needs to scrub the table.'

Jessica finished up the last of her Cheerios. 'Piff,' she whispered. 'I think there's something here, in this house. I've been hearing voices, people asking me to help them.

And seeing things, like the wallpaper moving. And last night I felt somebody stroking my hair.'

'Whooh,' said Epiphany, rolling her eyes.

'So, what I'm saying is, why don't you stay this afternoon and we'll see if we can find out who these people are.'

'I don't know . . . we were supposed to go skating.'

'I need a witness, Piff. Otherwise people will think it's the bump on my head that's done it.'

'I'm not sure.'

'Well, why don't we both go skating, and then we'll both come back here.'

'Are you allowed?'

'Sure I'm allowed.'

'Allowed to do what?' asked Grannie, taking away her cereal bowl.

'I'm allowed to go skating, aren't I? I'll wear my thick woolly hat in case I fall over.'

'You know what Dr Leeming said. Plenty of rest.'

'I've had plenty of rest. What I need now is plenty of exercise.'

'All right then. But you be careful. I had a boyfriend who nearly drowned in Millard's Pond.'

Under the Ice

The pond was already crowded when they arrived. It was almost a third of a mile across, frozen white, with crackly frozen reeds all around its edges and snow-laden trees overhanging it on three sides. Twenty or thirty Jeeps and Landcruisers were parked along the roadside, and dozens of people of all ages were spinning, circling and ice-dancing. The afternoon air was so frigid that their voices sounded oddly flat.

Jessica was wearing a shaggy red woolen hat, a white puffa jacket and red woolen tights. Epiphany wore a yellow jacket so bright that Jessica said it would melt the ice. They had been collected from the house by the mother of one of Epiphany's best friends, Dianna, in her brand-new Jeep. On the way to the pond, Jessica had sat in the front passenger seat next to Dianna's mother while Epiphany, Dianna and another friend, Whitney, had giggled in the back.

Dianna's mother was very slim and elegant, with a fake-leopardskin coat, long red fingernails and lots of gold rings, and she smelled of Giorgio. 'That your grandmother?' she asked as Jessica waved goodbye.

Jessica nodded. 'My parents were killed in a car accident. It was a year ago next month.'

'I'm so sorry to hear that. You must miss them dreadfully.'

'Yes.'

41

'I lost my mother in the summer, you know, and I miss her, too. But do you know something? I feel like she's never very far away. I don't know whether you feel the same.'

'Sometimes.'

'I was upstairs in the bedroom yesterday and I was straightening the bed when I felt her lay a hand on my shoulder. I knew it was her. I turned around, and I was almost expecting to see her standing there, but of course she wasn't.'

Jessica didn't answer. They had almost reached the pond, and Dianna's mother was slowing down. Then, as she was just about to park, Jessica said, 'Last night, my mother stroked my hair.'

Dianna's mother stopped the Jeep and stared at her. 'You really felt it?'

Jessica nodded.

'Then it's true, isn't it?' said Dianna's mother. 'They're not very far away, are they? They're still with us, you know. They're still so close!'

They skated close together, the four of them, chattering and laughing. Even though Epiphany and her friends were only thirteen, they accepted Jessica into their circle immediately, as long as she didn't mind talking about the latest Barbie accessories, and how cool it was to have a cellphone, and which boys in the eighth grade were really dreamy.

They skated all the way across the pond and under the trees, flashing from sunshine to shadow and back into sunshine. Jessica skated faster and faster, swooping around Epiphany and her friends and then spinning on the points of her skates. On the ice, it didn't matter if she had a limp, and she had always been a good skater. Her father used to take her skating regularly at Rockefeller Center.

She took hold of Epiphany's hand and helped her to pick up speed across the pond, and whirled her around like an ice-ballerina. Then she made all of the girls hold hands together, and they skated in a circle, faster and faster, round and round, all the way across the pond, until Epiphany tripped and they all tumbled over on the ice, laughing.

Jessica knelt on the ice on her hands and knees, gasping for breath. But as she tried to stand up, she thought she glimpsed something under the ice, something pale.

'Jessica! Come on, Jessica!' called Epiphany. 'Let's do it again!'

But Jessica was staring in growing horror at the blurred, oval shape that she could see beneath the ice. It looked like a face – a face that was wide-eyed with panic.

'Help me.'

She heard the words as distinctly as if they were being whispered right into her ear, even with all the shouting, laughing and whooping from the other skaters on the pond.

'Help me. It's coming to get us. It's going to take us all.'

Urgently, Jessica scraped away the fine crust of snow on top of the ice to clear a window. She looked down again, and the face was still there, pleading with her. And with a shiver, she recognized who it was. It was the same face that she had discovered in the attic, the boy with the rounded forehead and the long nose.

She hit the ice with her fist, twice, but all she did was hurt her fingers.

'Help!' she screamed, awkwardly climbing to her feet. 'Here! Help! There's somebody trapped under the ice!'

At first nobody took any notice. A middle-aged couple glided past her and simply shrugged at each other. But then she skated over to a large brown-bearded man who was teaching two little children to balance on the ice.

'You have to help me! There's somebody trapped under the ice!'

'What?' he said. 'Where?'

He called his wife over to take care of the children, and then he came skating after her. Jessica took him to the place where she had fallen over and knelt down. 'He was here! I saw his face! I heard him calling out for help!'

Two or three more men gathered around. 'What's going on, Daniel?'

'Girl here says that somebody's gotten themselves trapped under the ice.'

'I saw his face! I heard him calling for help!'

The bearded man knelt on the ice next to her and started to clear it with the side of his glove. 'Can't see nothing.'

'He coulda floated further in.'

'There's no current, though. He couldn't have floated far.'

'He'll be drowned by now, won't he?'

'Not if there's air between the ice and the water. That sometimes happens. He couldn't have called out for help otherwise.'

'Where'd he fall in? There's no holes in the ice any-where.'

'That doesn't matter, we'll have to get him out. Jay – there's an ax in the back of my truck.'

'I've got a snow shovel.'

'Me too.'

'We'll have to clear everybody off the pond.'

Five or six men ran off to their vehicles to bring shovels, tire irons and anything else they could use to break the ice, while several others shepherded everybody else up onto the banks.

Jessica stood back while the bearded man swung his ax and chipped into the ice. He swung again and again, grunting with every swing. At last the ice let out a squeaking crack, and a large triangular lump was broken away. Now all of the men started banging and hacking at it, and within a few

minutes a large jagged hole had been made, where there was
nothing but chilly black water.

The bearded man knelt at the edge of the ice and peered
downward, shading his eyes. He even swished his arm in
the water, to see if he could feel anything.

'Nothing so far. Let's chop her back a bit . . . he could
have floated toward the center.'

They hacked away at the ice for almost twenty minutes,
until cracks began to spread all across the pond and they
had to retreat to the edge.

'I couldn't see nothing at all,' said the bearded man,
sweating and shivering at the same time. 'Are you sure
there was somebody there?'

'I think we ought to call the Sheriff,' said one of the men.
'They need to send a diver down there.'

'I saw him,' said Jessica. 'I promise you, I saw him. He
was calling out, "Help me, help me."'

Dianna's mother came over; Epiphany had called her on
her cellphone: 'Jessica, are you all right?'

'I saw somebody under the ice, I promise.'

'That's OK. Listen, come and sit in the car, you're
freezing.'

'You won't take her away, ma'am, will you?' said the
bearded man. 'The Sheriff'll be wanting to talk to her.'

The Sheriff called just before supper that evening. He was
so tall that he had to duck his head when he came into the
kitchen. He had a big blue chin and a large nose but tiny,
glittering eyes like a raccoon.

'We dragged the pond from one end to the other, and all
we found was a 'seventy-six Chevy pick-up and a whole
tangle of lumber. I'm pleased to say that there was nobody
trapped under the ice, but I don't think the skaters were too
happy about it.'

Jessica was sitting at the far end of the kitchen table, with

Grandpa Willy beside her. 'Jessica says she saw somebody's face and heard them calling out for help and I for one believe her.'

'I'm not saying she's lying, Mr Williams, but I think it's pretty obvious that she was mistaken. Maybe it was your own face you saw, Jessica, reflected in the ice? It was a pretty bright morning, after all.'

'It was a boy. I heard his voice. He was calling for help.'

'I understand you had a pretty bad knock on the head last week.'

'It's nothing to do with that. I saw him with my own eyes. I heard him.'

'Well,' said the Sheriff, 'there's really nothing else I can do, except file a report.'

'Thank you, Sheriff,' said Grannie. 'You're sure you don't want some coconut cookies to take home?'

'No, thanks all the same. I just hope Jessica makes a rapid recovery, that's all.'

'Good-night, Sheriff.'

That evening, as they sat in the dining-room over a candlelit supper, Jessica took a deep breath and said, 'Grandpa?'

Grandpa Willy looked up from his ham and greens. 'What is it, honey?'

'Grandpa, I went up into the attic.'

He chewed and swallowed and then he said, 'You did, huh? Didn't I tell you, you really shouldn't go up there? The floor's only half boarded over, and it's not too safe. Wouldn't like you falling through the ceiling and ending up in bed with us!'

'I'm sorry, but I thought I heard a noise.'

'What kind of a noise?'

'I don't know. Maybe it was nothing. But it sounded like voices.'

Grandpa Willy looked across at Grannie. It was difficult for Jessica to see Grannie's face because of the candles that were shining in the middle of the table.

Grannie said, 'Is that the reason you asked me if there were any children in the house?'

'That's right.' Jessica didn't know if she was making a serious mistake, asking Grannie and Grandpa Willy about what she had heard. Supposing there *were* children trapped in the house somewhere, and supposing Grannie and Grandpa Willy were keeping them captive? But when she really thought about it, it was too much like 'Hansel and Gretel' to be true.

Grandpa Willy forked himself another boiled potato out of the tureen. 'These old houses, they always make noises. It's the wind, mostly, blowing down the chimneys, and under the floorboards. The plumbing, too.'

Jessica said, 'I went right down to the end of the attic and I found some masks.'

Grandpa Willy nodded. 'I see. You didn't disturb them or nothing?'

'Oh, no. I just looked at them. They scared me when I first saw them. I thought they were real children.'

'We never quite knew what to do about those,' said Grannie. 'We thought about taking them to the New Milford Historical Society Museum, but somehow we thought it was more fitting if we left them where we found them.'

'Do you know who they are?'

'Oh, yes. They were the Pennington children. The Penningtons used to live in this house before my father bought it. What all the children's names were, I can't remember, but they're written down someplace.'

'What happened to them?'

'They went down with the Rocky Mountain spotted fever. There was kind of an epidemic of it in this part of the country just before World War Two. Usually kids get over it, but this

47

was a real bad strain, and they never did. The oldest child was fifteen and the youngest was four and all five of them died within a week.'

'That's terrible.'

'Yes, it was,' said Grandpa Willy. 'The children's parents were spared, but of course they were grief-struck, and they never got over it. They had a death mask made of every child, so that they could remember what they looked like. But from what I was told the mother disappeared and the father just stayed in bed all day drinking and the house went to rack and ruin, and that's why my father was able to buy it so cheap. My father couldn't really afford it, and neither can your grandmother and me, but it's our home, and we plan on spending the rest of our days here. But I guess in a way it's those children's home, too, and that's why we left those masks where they were.'

'That face I saw under the ice, at Millard's Pond . . . that looked like one of the death masks.'

Grandpa Willy reached across the tablecloth and held her hand. 'I'm not saying for one moment that you didn't see what you thought you saw. I told the Sheriff that I believed you were telling the God's-honest truth, and I believe you were. But, more often than not, things aren't what they appear to be.'

Grannie said, 'Do you want some more greens, sweetie-pie?'

Jessica lay awake staring at the ceiling. Supposing the knock on her head *had* made her go peculiar? After all, she had never heard the voices before she was concussed, and she had never seen the wallpaper move. Yet she was certain that she had felt somebody stroking her hair, and that she had seen a flower on the wallpaper flutter. And she was just as sure that she had seen the boy beneath the ice, his mouth opening and closing as he desperately struggled to breathe.

In the middle of the night, it started snowing again, thick and silent. Jessica slept with one hand against the wall, her fingers half open. She dreamed that a pale yellowish hand came sliding out of the wallpaper. It stroked her palm, then intertwined its fingers with hers, and gently started to tug her toward the wall.

She suddenly woke up, and she could actually feel the fingers tugging her, and she cried out, 'No!' and whipped her hand away from the wall. She sat up for a long time, breathing shallow and fast, massaging her hand and staring at the wallpaper.

It had been a dream, hadn't it? It must have been a dream. But all the same, she climbed out of bed and curled up instead on her basketwork chair. She woke up very early the next morning with pins-and-needles in her feet and a creaking neck.

Diamonds and Wolves

G rannie made her a breakfast of hot waffles with maple syrup and blueberry jelly, and a big mug of hot chocolate with three spoonfuls of sugar in. 'Are you all right, sweetie-pie?' she asked. 'You look a mite tired.'

'I didn't sleep so well, that's all.'

'You didn't hear any more voices?'

'No. But I couldn't stop thinking about those Pennington children.'

'I know. It's so sad, isn't it? But things were a whole lot different in those days. Lots of children died of all kinds of quite ordinary illnesses like measles and chicken-pox. When I was a young girl there wasn't any such thing as antibiotics.'

Jessica washed her plate and her mug. Then she went into the hallway and put on her long black hooded overcoat, her long black scarf and her bright red Wellingtons. She called out, 'Goodbye, Grannie, see you later!' and went out of the house into the snow. It was always quiet out here on the road to Allen's Corners, but today the hills were so silent that Jessica felt she was deaf.

She walked to old Mrs Crawford's house, which was a quarter of a mile nearer to town. It stood behind a broken-down picket fence, surrounded by the wildest of gardens: a small single-story building with a sagging roof and a verandah cluttered with broken chairs, bunches of dried flowers and a rusting barbecue. Jessica went up to the front door and knocked. The tarnished brass knocker was cast in the shape of a snarling wolf, and Jessica often wondered why Mrs Crawford had chosen something so scary.

Mrs Crawford came to the door, her golden Labrador Sebastian almost choking himself with his leash. She was a small woman with steel-gray hair cut into a bob, and although her face was wrinkled Jessica could tell by her wide green eyes and her distinctive cheekbones that once upon a time she must have been strikingly beautiful. A purple shawl was knotted untidily around her shoulders, and she wore a shapeless black woolen dress and extraordinary black high-heeled shoes. 'Ah, Jessica, thank goodness. I only have to say, "Jessica's coming" and Sebastian goes hysterical, don't you, Sebastian, you over-excitable idiot?'

'I'll take him round Boardman's Farm,' said Jessica.

'That would be wonderful. Don't fall into a snowdrift, that's all I ask. I don't want to have to come looking for you with a team of huskies and a shovel.'

Jessica took Sebastian's leash and wound it around her hand. Sebastian barked and jumped and his tail slapped furiously against the door-frame. 'How are you feeling?' said Mrs Crawford. 'Still have headaches?'

'I'm better, thanks. I should be able to go back to school next week.'

Mrs Crawford was about to close the door when she frowned and said, 'Something's disturbing you, Jessica.'

'I'm fine, really. Down, Sebastian! There's a good boy.'

'No, I can feel it. You're worried about something, I don't know what.'

'Honestly, I'm not worried about anything at all.'

'You can't fool me, Jessica. I can see your aura as plain as the nose on your face. And your aura's muddy.'

Jessica tilted her head in bewilderment.

'Everybody has an aura, Jessica. At your age, it should sparkle like the stars. But yours is definitely muddy.'

'What does that mean?'

'It means that you're troubled. It means that you're worried about something and you don't know how to resolve it. Am I speaking the truth?'

'Well, yes, I guess so, in a way.'

'Why don't you take Sebastian for his walk, and then when you come back I can find out what it is that's bothering you.'

'All right.'

Mrs Crawford laid a hand on her arm. 'I promise you, Jessica, whatever it is, there's always a way.'

Jessica crossed the glassy white road and forced open the five-bar gate that would take her to the south-east meadow of Boardman's Farm. All the cattle were kept in the cowshed in this weather, and so she was able to unclip Sebastian's leash and let him run madly from one end of the field to the other, bounding over frozen tussocks and leaping explosively through snow-covered bushes.

On the far side of the field the naked trees stuck up like witches' broomsticks, and behind them the sun was nothing but a wan yellow disk.

Jessica was crossing toward the woods when she heard somebody calling her. She turned around and saw Epiphany running toward her, waving.

'I called at your house,' Epiphany panted. 'Your granny said you might be here.'

'Oh . . . I'm only taking Mrs Crawford's dog for a walk.'

'Can I come too?'

'All right. If you don't mind walking with a mad person.'

'You're not mad.'

'The Sheriff seems to think I am. So does everybody else.'

'The Sheriff is a typical patronizing male authority figure who has as much imagination as a pretzel.'

'Where'd you learn that?'

'I read it in a book called *The Self-Respecting Woman* by Sherma Katzenbaum.'

'You read books like that?'

'Of course. The trouble with most women is that they only read romances about swooning heroines who fall in love with disreputable rogues, or books about neurotic thirty-somethings who keep worrying about their weight and can't find boyfriends. They don't understand that you can only get power over men by treating yourself with unwavering respect.'

'I was still reading fairy stories when I was your age. Well, I still do now.'

'Fairy stories are all right. They're a celebration of the essential mysticism of the female psyche.'

'Oh.'

They entered the woods, with Sebastian tearing away from them, and then tearing back again, his pink tongue steaming. Frozen twigs crackled under their boots, and four or five loons flurried up from the pond beyond the trees.

Epiphany swung a stick. 'Did you really see a face under the ice?'

'About as clearly as I can see you now.'

'Do you think somebody's trying to get through to you?'

'What do you mean?'

'Well, you talked about another world, like Fairyland, right next to this world. It seems like somebody from that world wants to talk to you. You've heard voices, haven't you? And you've seen a golf bag that looked like a dog and a lamp that looked like a man.'

'I don't know. I'm beginning to think it's all in my head.'

They circled the pond and walked back along the track

53

that led to the main farm gate. Epiphany sang, 'I like bread and butter . . . I like toast and jam . . . that's what my baby feeds me . . . 'cause he's my loving man' in such a shrill, high-pitched voice that Jessica had to clamp her gloves over her ears. When they arrived at Mrs Crawford's house, Mrs Crawford said, 'You're coming in, aren't you? I can put some brownies in the microwave.'

'Oh yes please,' said Jessica immediately. She always liked going into Mrs Crawford's house, not because of her microwaved brownies, which were invariably gooey, but because of all the arcane clutter that filled the hallway and the living-room: cuckoo clocks and totem poles and statuettes of naked dancers, umbrellas and stuffed cockatoos and strange pictures of people in evening dress, floating through the air.

'This is Epiphany,' said Jessica. 'I call her Piff. She's a feminist.'

'Well, that's wonderful,' said Mrs Crawford. 'I always think that all of us ought to have some kind of cause, even if it's nothing more than free walking-sticks for the elderly. Here –' she picked a heap of women's magazines from the worn-out brown corduroy couch, and dropped them onto the worn-out carpet – 'do sit down, and I'll put the brownies on to ping.'

Jessica and Epiphany took off their coats and sat side by side on the couch. It was warm in Mrs Crawford's house, almost uncomfortably warm. A log fire was burning fiercely in the cast-iron grate, and it wasn't long before Sebastian came trotting in from the kitchen and flopped himself down in front of it. He smelled strongly of steaming dog.

'Poor Sebastian,' said Mrs Crawford, as she came back in. 'I think you've exhausted him.'

Epiphany looked around at the tall vases filled with dyed-gold pampas grass, the boxes of jigsaws and the porcelain busts of inanely smiling girls. Over the fireplace hung a large dark oil painting which depicted a woman in a black cloak emerging from a solid oak door, as if she had walked right through it, like a ghost.

'That's called "The Appearance of Eve",' said Mrs Crawford. 'It was painted by a Dutchman who went mad shortly afterward, Jan van der Hoeven. He always swore that it was painted from life.'

'I'm not surprised he went mad,' said Jessica.

'But you're not mad,' Epiphany reassured her.

'I'm beginning to wonder.'

'Why should you think you're mad?' asked Mrs Crawford.

Jessica shrugged and said nothing, but Epiphany said, 'She's been hearing voices, and seeing the flowers on her wallpaper move.'

'Piff!' Jessica protested. 'You promised you wouldn't tell anybody!'

'Never mind,' Mrs Crawford reassured her. 'I'm not just anybody, am I? Where do these voices come from? What do they sound like?'

'They sound like children. They keep saying, "help us, help us, it's coming to get us, we're all going to be taken." At first I thought they were coming from another bedroom, and then I thought they were coming down the chimney. I looked up in the attic, everywhere, but I couldn't find them. It's almost as if—'

'Yes? It's almost as if what?'

Jessica didn't want to say, but Epiphany nudged her. 'Go on, Jessica. Tell her.'

Jessica hesitated for a moment, but at last she blurted out, 'It's stupid. It sounds like they're coming from the wall.'

'I see,' said Mrs Crawford, and she looked quite serious. 'Can you tell how many children there are?'

'No, they all talk together.'

Mrs Crawford thought about that for a while, and then

she said, 'You say you have wallpaper . . . what kind of a pattern is it?'

'Flowers . . . roses and irises and thistles.'

'Well, I want to show you something, and then I think you'll realize that you're not stupid and you're certainly not mad.'

She went over to a desk with a glass-fronted bookcase on top of it, crammed higgledy-piggledy with all kinds of books and papers and folded-up newspapers. She rummaged in one of the drawers for a while, then came back with a sheet of cardboard in her hand.

'I thought something was worrying you, didn't I? I can always tell. My mother used to say that I had gipsy blood in me. I don't know why: my father ran a radio-repair business, and my grandfather was a dentist – hardly what you'd call Romany stock. 'Here,' she said, squashing herself onto the couch right next to Jessica. 'What do you see on this piece of cardboard?'

Jessica frowned at it. All she could see was a pattern like interwoven string, fastened at intervals with decorative knots.

'It's like some kind of weaving,' she suggested.

'Yes, that's right. But keep staring at it, and see if it turns into anything else.'

Jessica stared at it and stared at it, but the pattern didn't change. It began to shift slightly in front of her eyes, but that was only because she was staring at it so intently.

'Do you see the knot in the middle?' asked Mrs Crawford. 'What I want you to do is hook your finger around it.'

'I don't know what you mean.'

'Hook your finger around it, all the way around it, and pull it.'

'But I can't. It's only a picture.'

'Try.'

Jessica hesitated, but then she stuck out her right index

finger and moved it nearer and nearer to the pattern, until it was almost touching the cardboard.

'Go on,' Mrs Crawford encouraged her.

She pushed her finger forward, and to her astonishment she was able to push it right into the pattern, as if the piece of cardboard wasn't flat at all but a three-dimensional box criss-crossed with knotted string. She curled her finger around the knot in the middle, and she was able to pull it outward. She could actually feel its tension, as if it were real string.

'There now,' said Mrs Crawford. Jessica withdrew her finger, and Mrs Crawford turned the pattern over to show her that it was still mounted on nothing more than a flat piece of cardboard.

'How do you do that?' asked Jessica. 'Piff – did you see that?'

'I saw it all right,' said Piff, in an awed voice. 'That's some conjuring trick, right?'

'Ah, but it isn't a conjuring trick,' said Mrs Crawford. 'What I'm trying to prove to you is that you were quite right to wonder if the voices came from the wall.'

She stood up; and put the pattern down on the table. 'There is another world, a world of patterns, where what you see is what there is. It's no more complicated than that. If a pattern looks as if you can hook your finger round it, you can. Do you ever see faces in your wallpaper?'

'In the roses sometimes.'

'I thought you might. Roses are always rather face-like, aren't they? But in the world inside your wallpaper, they actually do have faces. In the world inside your wallpaper, or your curtains, or your carpets, everything is exactly what you perceive it to be.'

'There's really a world there? Really?'

'Some people say that it's the world we originally came from. They say that we decorate our homes and our clothes with patterns because they remind us of the world we once lived in.'

'You mean we can get through, from one world into the other?'

'Within limits. You hooked your finger round the knot, didn't you? Where do you think your finger actually was, when you stuck it into that pattern? It didn't come out of the back of the cardboard, did it? It wasn't here, in this room. It was there, Jessica, in the world of patterns. Look.'

Mrs Crawford knelt down on the green-and-yellow carpet, which was patterned with stylized waterlilies and curly leaves. She stared at it for almost a minute, and then she scooped her hand into it, actually into it, and lifted it up again, with one of the waterlilies in the palm of her hand.

'Whoa, that has to be a trick,' said Epiphany. 'No way you can do that for real.'

'Feel it,' said Mrs Crawford, and handed her the woven-wool waterlily. Epiphany turned it over and over, then shook her head in perplexity and handed it back.

'How do you know about this?' asked Jessica.

Mrs Crawford replaced the waterlily, smoothed it over, and seamlessly it became part of the carpet again.

'If that's not a conjuring trick, that must be real magic,' said Epiphany.

Mrs Crawford smiled. 'No – I don't believe in magic. But I do believe in other worlds – worlds that exist on the other side of mirrors, or reflected in ponds, or in wallpaper patterns.'

She stood up and went to the window. The wintry light made her look very pale, as if she were a ghost of herself. 'In fact, I *know* there are other worlds. I've known it since I was seven years old. They had a science conference in San Diego about five years ago and all of these eminent physicists said that there must be alternative realities, alongside "our" reality. And that was such a relief, because all of my life I had thought that I must have been imagining what happened to me, even though I was convinced that I wasn't.'

The Sapphire Ring

'It was in the winter of 1937. In those days, believe it or not, I used to live in your grandparents' house. My mother was working as cook and housekeeper for George and Martha Pennington, and so she and I had rooms upstairs. In November I went down with a fever and I had to stay in bed for nearly three days. My bedroom had wallpaper with diamond shapes on it, and the more I stared at it, the more it looked like dozens and dozens of diamond-shaped faces.

'On the second night, just as I was going to sleep, I heard somebody talking to me, a woman. She called me by name, "Edwina! Edwina!" I was frightened at first, but then I heard singing. Sweet, sweet singing, so sweet that it would make you cry. And still this woman's voice calling, "Edwina!"

'I switched on my light and all around the room the pattern on the wallpaper was faces – still diamond shapes, but faces too – and the faces were singing to me. I sat up in bed and I could feel a wind blowing through my hair. It felt so cool, and it was strong enough to ruffle the pages of the magazine beside my bed.

'I climbed out of bed and I walked toward the wall on the opposite side of my bedroom. The singing didn't stop, and when I was close to the diamond shapes I could see the little purple squares that looked like eyes and the red circles that looked like mouths, and the eyes were looking at me and the mouths were moving.

'Then the space between the diamonds became a kind of

60

Hidden World

crooked arm, and the arm reached out of the wallpaper and took my hand. It drew me gently toward the wall, closer and closer, and then before I knew it I had passed right through the wallpaper and into the world that lay beyond it.'

'You really walked into the wall?' asked Jessica. She didn't know if Mrs Crawford was making it all up, but even if she was, she still wanted to know what had happened.

'I really walked into the wall,' said Mrs Crawford, crossing her heart with her finger.

'What did it feel like?'

'It felt like . . . I don't know. It felt like walking through very soft tissue paper, that's all. I found myself standing in an empty room, and it was so bright in there that I could hardly see. The walls were the same color as the wallpaper in my own bedroom, except that here, on the other side of the wallpaper, the diamond shapes actually floated in the air, all around me. The singing went on and on, and for some reason it made me feel very happy.'

'You don't think you were dreaming?'

'Oh, no. This wasn't like a dream at all. I could still feel the wind and I could still hear the woman calling, "Edwina!" The diamond shapes flew all round my head like clouds of butterflies, and they guided me across the room toward the door.

'I opened the door. Outside there was a flat white desert that looked as if it stretched for miles and miles. I could see diamond-shaped mountains on the horizon, and bushes with diamond-shaped leaves. I went through the door, and I started to walk, and all the time the diamond patterns kept fluttering all around me.

'The singing died away, and after that the desert was completely silent. I felt as if I was walking for hours and hours, although I couldn't have been. After a while I saw a small figure walking toward me. It was a woman, wearing a dark rusty-colored cloak. She came up to me and laid her

61

hands on my shoulders. Her cloak had a big floppy hood, so that most of her face was hidden, but I could see that she was smiling, in a sad sort of way.

'She said, "I've been waiting for you, Edwina. I've been waiting for somebody for so many years. I want you to tell Mrs Pennington that I'm still here." I asked her who she was, but all she did was take a small sapphire ring off her finger and give it to me. "She'll know," she said. But then she said, "You should hurry away now, it can be very dangerous here." She turned and pointed toward the horizon. I could just see dozens of black shapes, running toward us. They looked like a pack of wolves.

'The woman took hold of my hand and led me back to the door. We seemed to get there in no time at all. It was so strange: the door stood in the desert with nothing around it at all, just a door. But when she opened it, we stepped back into the empty room. The old lady said, "God bless," and she kissed her fingertips and touched me on the forehead, I'll never forget that. Then I went back through the wallpaper and there I was, standing in my bedroom again. It was seven o'clock in the morning and it was just beginning to grow light.

'I felt very tired and weak, but my fever had broken, and I was over the worst.'

'Did you tell Mrs Pennington? Did you give her the ring?'

'Yes, I did.'

'Was she pleased?'

'Not . . . at all. For some reason she was very angry with me. She said that I was making up cruel stories and that I must have stolen the ring from her jewelry box. She said I was never to talk about it again, or else she'd have me arrested for being a thief and a liar.'

'Did you never find out why?'

Mrs Crawford shook her head.

'Did you try to do it again?' asked Epiphany. 'Go through the wallpaper, I mean?'

'I did it once more, but I had been moved to another bedroom then, with green wallpaper that looked like thorn bushes. When I went through it was very dark and there were some horrible prickly shapes in the darkness, and believe me they gave me a very bad fright. I couldn't get out of there quickly enough.'

'And you've never tried to do it again since then?'

'Some things are best left as memories, or puzzles. In any case, a short time after that, all of the Pennington children got sick and died and Mrs Pennington let my mother go. We moved to live with my aunt in Darien and I never went back to that house again.'

'That's sad.'

'Yes, it was. They were such lovely children. But it was a long time ago now.'

'Do you think I could walk into my wallpaper?'

'As far as I know, anybody can do it, given the right amount of belief, and the right kind of wallpaper pattern. But I wouldn't recommend that you try it. The usual rules of nature obviously don't apply, and who knows what scary things you might find there? Those prickly things, for instance, or those creatures that looked like wolves.'

'So what do you think I ought to do?'

'About your voices, you mean? I don't think you should do anything. Whoever they are, whatever they are, I don't see how you can possibly help them. If they're facing some kind of danger, you'd have to face it too.'

The Leaves of Memory

On Tuesday morning, Grandpa Willy drove her to Dr Leeming's clinic in his old green Pontiac. Dr Leeming was bald but very handsome, with sharp blue eyes and minty-smelling breath. He removed the stitches very carefully, but Jessica still heard a noise inside her head like wool being pulled through cardboard.

When he had finished he swabbed her cut and stuck a clean dressing on it. Then he gave her an eye test and made her place differently shaped bricks into a pattern, to test her co-ordination.

'Well, young lady, I think you're ready to go back on active service,' he told her. 'You haven't been having any headaches, have you? How about your memory? Can you remember the day when you fell downstairs?'

'Mostly. I can't remember actually falling, but I can remember everything else.'

'Have you had any unusual reactions? For instance, have you seen things that you don't normally see?'

Jessica felt herself blushing. 'No . . . nothing like that.'

'Sometimes, when they've suffered a concussion, people see shadows out of the corner of their eye. Or flashes of light. Sometimes they even think they hear voices. You haven't experienced anything like that?'

'No,' said Jessica, even though she felt guilty about lying. But Renko had heard the voices too, so they couldn't be anything to do with her knocking her head.

'Okey-dokey,' said Dr Leeming. 'But if you have any more headaches, or you feel nauseous, or if you experience any other symptoms, you come see me pronto, all right?'

As they left the clinic Grandpa Willy said, 'How about a cheeseburger with everything on it?'

'I didn't think Grannie let you eat cheeseburgers. What about your blood pressure?'

Grandpa Willy gave her hand an affectionate squeeze. 'One cheeseburger isn't going to kill me. Besides, we all have to go to the Great Beyond one day, so what's the point of denying yourself an occasional unhealthy treat?'

When they were sitting next to the steamed-up window in Clark's Burger Bar, eating cheeseburgers and sharing a basket of French fries, Jessica said, 'Do you believe in heaven, Grandpa?'

'What, with cherubs and clouds and all that caboodle?'

'I don't actually mean angels and harps and stuff. I mean an actual place that we go to, when we die.'

'Well, yes, I think I do. Some folks say that because you don't remember nothing before you was born, that proves for a fact that you don't experience nothing when you turn your toes up. But that's like saying that just because there wasn't any picture of fairies before you drew it, it stops existing after you've crumpled it up and thrown it in the fire. It still exists in here, in your head, doesn't it?, and it still exists in the heads of anybody who might have seen it. So long as there are people who remember you, then I believe that you're still alive. Maybe you pass into infinity once there's nobody left alive who knew you, and maybe that's the way God makes sure that heaven doesn't get too crowded.

'But I believe that your mom and dad are in heaven, because you think about them still, don't you? They're still in your heart, and what sweeter place could there be than that?'

Jessica carefully extricated the pickle from her cheese-burger.

'I'll have that,' said Grandpa Willy. 'They give me the force-ten wind, but what the heck.'

'Do you think dead people can talk to us?' asked Jessica.

'What's brought this on? You're talking mighty existential today.'

'It's these voices I keep hearing.'

Grandpa Willy laid his hand on top of hers. His skin was like crumpled tissue paper. 'Sometimes our minds play some rare tricks on us, sweetheart. I used to have an old black-and-white spotty dog called Captain when I was a boy, and Captain died of distemper. But I swear to you that when I was walking along the road one morning, I saw him trotting ahead of me, as plain as day. I've never told anybody that before, in case they thought I was screwy. But whether he was really there or not, I saw him all right.'

He sat back and smiled at her. 'If you hear these voices again, you call me, and then we'll find out if I can hear them too. Now, how about one of those giant ice-cream sundaes with all the sprinkle-sprankles on top?'

That night, Jessica stayed awake so late that she heard the grandfather clock chiming one o'clock in the hall below. She had bought a small blue plastic flashlight of her own, and every now and then she shone it on the wallpaper to see if it was moving. But the roses, irises and blessed thistles didn't stir, and she heard nobody calling for help.

At half past one she turned over, pulled the comforter up over her shoulders, and fell asleep. She dreamed that her mother was downstairs, in the kitchen. She could hear her singing, but all she could see was her back, with her apron strings dangling down. It must have been early fall: even though the sun was shining through the open kitchen door, the first dried-up beech leaves were rattling across the yard outside.

She tried to say, 'Mom?' but for some reason her mouth wouldn't work, and she couldn't make her legs carry her into the kitchen. The sun died away, and it grew chilly and dark The wind rose, and the beech leaves started to blow into the kitchen, scattering across the floor.

Jessica cried out, 'Mom!' but she knew that her mother couldn't hear her, and she began to weep with frustration.

She woke up. Her bedroom was filled with sunshine. She propped herself up on one elbow, and there was a crackling noise. Her bed was covered with coppery, curled-up leaves.

Slowly, carefully, she climbed out of bed and stood staring at them. You can dream of leaves. You can dream of cats and cakes and bright red bouncy balls. But you don't expect to wake up in the morning to find a cat sleeping on the pillow next to you, or a cake on your nightstand, or a ball bouncing its way across your bedroom carpet.

She wondered if she ought to call Grandpa Willy to come and have a look, but in the end she decided not to. After all, he wasn't very well, what with his angina and his high blood pressure, and she didn't want to upset him.

She put all the leaves in her waste-paper basket, then went downstairs for an early breakfast.

Pretty Face, Ugly Heart

The schoolyard was crowded with running, shouting children, and snowballs were flying everywhere, even though Principal Tucker had banned them as 'offensive weapons'. One snowball exploded on Jessica's shoulder and another smacked her in the back. She stooped down and made one herself, but she was no good at throwing and it only hit the wall.

'Gimpy couldn't hit a barn door,' mocked Sue-Anne. She was sitting on her favorite perch, the top of the wooden box that covered the ventilator, from where she could queen it over everybody in the schoolyard. She was wearing a white parka with a real fox-fur hood, and her hair was a cascade of golden curls.

Her courtiers were standing around her: Charlene, Micky, Fay and Renko, as well as Elica, a pretty, dark-skinned Romanian girl whose parents had come to America seeking political asylum. Elica spoke little English and Mrs Walker had charged Sue-Anne with taking care of her, although Sue-Anne's idea of 'taking care' of anybody was to make them run endless errands for her, and give her money when she was short.

'Back at school, then, Gimpy?' asked Sue-Anne. 'Let's hope you've had some sense knocked into you.'

'Why don't you leave me alone?' Jessica challenged her. 'I've never done anything to you.'

'I can't leave you alone because you're always there,

that's why. Always limping around, trying to make everybody feel sorry for you.'

'I don't need anybody to feel sorry for me. I think people ought to feel sorry for *you*, if you've got nothing better to do than make yourself obnoxious.'

'Oh, believe me, Jessica, there is nothing on this planet more obnoxious than looking at you. Now that's enough to make anybody want to barf.'

'You're ridiculous,' Jessica retorted. 'Look at you, sitting up there with all of your stooges around you. You look like Goldilocks and the Five Bears.'

'You can't talk to me like that!' snapped Sue-Anne. 'At least I don't limp around like the Hunchback of Notre Dame!'

The school doors opened and everybody shuffled inside. Mr Kurtzman, the Deputy Principal, was standing on the steps and he smiled at Jessica and said, 'How are you feeling, Jessica? Good to have you back. I've just had details of a statewide art competition . . . remind me to give them to you. I think one of your fairy pictures could stand a good chance of winning.'

Jessica went to her locker, took off her coat and collected her books. As she did so, somebody pulled out the neck of her sweater at the back and crammed a handful of snow down it.

She cried out, 'Oww!' and frantically tried to shake the snow out of her clothes. On the other side of the corridor, Sue-Anne was clapping her hands and laughing, while Micky was brushing snow off his sleeves. 'Snow nice to have you back!' Charlene taunted.

Calvin ducked around Jessica and snatched her lunchbox out of her locker. 'Here!' he said. 'Let's see what gimps put in their sandwiches! Bet they eat limp lettuce leaves! Get it, *limp* lettuce leaves!'

'Here!' said Sue-Anne, and Calvin tossed the lunchbox

across to her. She opened it up, and Jessica's orange fell out and rolled across the floor. Micky stamped on it, and said, 'That's one thing that gimps have for lunch! Fresh-squeezed orange!'

Sue-Anne unwrapped the paper napkins around Jessica's sandwiches. 'Oh my God, look at this! How disgusting! They look like they're filled with vomit!'

Charlene peered into the box. 'You're right! It is vomit! The gimp has vomit sandwiches for lunch . . . saves her the trouble of barfing afterwards!'

'They're tuna-mayonnaise and give them back,' said Jessica, pushing Micky to one side. Sue-Anne skipped away, holding the lunchbox high over her head.

'You want them? You want your vomit sandwiches? You'll have to come get them!'

Jessica limped after her and snatched hold of her green cashmere sweater. 'Give them back!' she insisted. 'My grandmother made those!'

'Then it looks like your grandmother feels the same way about you that I do! Enough to make you puke!'

Jessica pulled harder at Sue-Anne's sweater and the seam under her arm tore apart. Sue-Anne screamed in indignation. 'Look what you've done! You animal! Look what you've done to my sweater! That cost nearly three hundred dollars at Saks!'

In a fury, she threw Jessica's sandwiches onto the floor, along with a cheese triangle and a Snickers bar. Jessica tried to save them, but Calvin and Micky kicked them around and then trod on them.

Sue-Anne, meanwhile, went to Jessica's locker and started to rip the pages out of one of her sketchbooks. 'You tear my things, I've got a right to tear yours!'

But it was then that Renko grabbed hold of Sue-Anne's wrist and tugged the sketchbook out of her hand.

'What do you think you're doing?' Sue-Anne demanded.

'Get your hands off me!'

'That's enough,' said Renko. 'Leave her alone.'

'What? Whose side are you on?'

'I'm on nobody's side. You've done enough, that's all.'

'Listen, you geek, I'll decide when I've done enough. If you think I'm going to put up with sharing the same building with some pathetic gimp who brings vomit sandwiches in for lunch, then you've got another think coming!'

'Yeah, what's the matter with you, Renko?' said Micky. 'You gone soft or something?'

'You want to find out how soft I'm not?' Renko warned him.

'So why are you standing up for the gimp all of a sudden?'

Renko pointed a finger at him. 'Her name is Jessica. If you even whisper the word "gimp" again, and I hear you, I'll punch your teeth right down your throat, braces and all.'

'Hey, man, why the hissy fit?'

'No hissy fit, Micky. All I'm doing is telling you that enough is enough. We almost killed Jessica last week and I'm as much to blame as the rest of you. I'm not going to make the rest of her life miserable just because Princess Sue-Anne is all eaten up with jealousy.'

'*Jealousy?*' screamed Sue-Anne. 'Did you hear that? Jealousy? You seriously think that I'm jealous of some ratty-haired weirdo who can't even walk straight?'

Renko went close up to Sue-Anne and stared her straight in the face.

'What?' she challenged him.

But without a word he reached into her open locker and picked up one of her brand-new white-and-silver Nike trainers. He held it up in front of her; she pouted at him defiantly. But then he lifted a pineapple-and-mango yogurt out of her lunchbox, pierced the foil top with his thumbnail, and slowly emptied the entire pot into her shoe. Sue-Anne stood with her mouth wide open, totally shocked.

'You just – you just – look what you just did!'

'You are a vain and very stupid person,' said Renko. 'Personally I don't care how vain and stupid you are, but you're not going to take your personality problems out on Jessica, or anybody else, ever again. You got me?'

Sue-Anne abruptly burst into tears. Without a word, she turned and flounced off along the corridor, leaving the rest of them standing amidst the squashed remains of Jessica's lunch.

Micky went off silently too. Calvin said, 'Hey, man,' and hunkered down to pick up the smashed sandwiches. Charlene bit her lip, then held out her hand to Jessica and said, 'Sorry. I'm sorry. I guess I never thought what I was doing.'

Elica had kept well away during the bullying, but now she stepped forward and opened her Tupperware lunchbox. 'Please, is for you share, yes? Is a pitta, with chicken. Also banana.'

'You can have some of mine, too,' said Renko. 'That's if you don't mind peanut butter and Twinkies.'

Elica said, 'I do not go with Sue-Anne more. In Romania we say, "*La chip frumos sila inimã gãunos.*" This means "a pretty face but an ugly heart". I am now a friend of you.'

Jessica still felt shaky, and the back of her sweater was soaked in chilly melted snow. She turned to Renko and took hold of his sleeve. 'Thank you. You didn't have to do that.'

'Hey, forget it. Sue-Anne's been giving me a right royal pain in the butt all semester. I'm only sorry I didn't stand up to her earlier.'

'Why don't you come round to my house after school?' Jessica suggested. 'You too, Elica. My grandmother's going to be making chicken pot-pie, and there's always far too much.'

'I know: you want us to go hunting for those mysterious kids again,' said Renko.

'I do want to talk to you about that,' said Jessica. 'And you won't believe what I found on my bed when I woke up this morning.'

Follow the Flowers

They sat around the kitchen table while Grannie served them heaped-up platefuls of chicken pot-pie and candied sweet potatoes, with two helpings of Rocky Road to follow. Afterward they helped Grannie to dry the dishes while Grandpa Willy told them tall stories about his days in the Marines. 'I could bite through barbed wire with my teeth!' Later they went up to Jessica's bedroom and chilled out.

Renko sat on the bed and sorted through Jessica's CD collection while Elica circled the room, smiling in delight at all the drawings of fairies and elves that she had pinned up on the walls.

'This little person, in Romania we call her a *zãna*. She will steal food, and jewels, also your baby, and give you instead her own baby.'

'Hey, this is cool,' said Renko, holding up a Limp Bizkit CD. 'You've got some really cool sounds here.'

'Just because I draw fairies and elves doesn't mean I have to listen to "The Dance of the Sugar Plum Fairy" all the time.'

'Anyhow,' said Renko, sniffing, 'what about these mystery kids? Don't tell me you found them?'

'Kind of.' She told him how she had explored the attic, and how she had found the five death masks.

'That is seriously creepy,' Renko put in. 'Mind you – my mom keeps my grandmother's false teeth in the bathroom, I don't know why, my grandmother died about three years ago. What does she think her teeth are going to do – start singing lullabies to her?'

'In Romania, when a child is dead, his best toy is keeped by his picture, for remember happy.'

Jessica told them about Mrs Crawford, too. 'Ah, she's nuts, that Mrs Crawford,' said Renko. 'My mom says she went batty after her husband died.'

Jessica picked up her wastebasket and held it right under Renko's nose. 'If she's nuts, what about this? Last night I dreamed that I could see my mom in the kitchen and in my dream some dead leaves blew in through the doorway. When I woke up – look.'

Renko scooped up a handful and scrunched them. 'OK, so you've got yourself a wastebasket full of leaves. How do I know you didn't get them out of the garden?'

'Because I didn't. They were all over my bed, I swear it. So where do you think they came from?'

'You think this leafs come from wall?' asked Elica. 'How is this?'

'I don't really understand it myself. But I keep hearing those voices, and when I was lying in bed I felt sure that I could feel somebody stroking my hair. Mrs Crawford said that there's another world, and you can step into it.'

'Well, that's one hell of a fascinating theory,' said Renko. 'But how exactly do you get into a solid wall?'

'Mrs Crawford said you only have to believe.'

'Oh, yes, like jumping off the top of the Empire State Building and believing that you can fly. You try walking into that wall and you're going to end up with nothing but a flat nose.' He squashed his hand against his face by way of illustration.

'It cannot be true,' Elica agreed.

Renko went back to rummaging through her CDs. When he glanced up and saw that she was still looking at him, he said, 'Go ahead. Be my guest. You want to walk into the wall, fine.'

'Maybe there are times when you can do it and times when you can't.'

'Oh, sure, and maybe my pet hamsters talk to each other when I'm out of the room.'

Although Renko was so skeptical about the existence of another world inside Jessica's wallpaper, they had a cheerful evening, and they were reduced to rib-aching laughter when they tried to teach Elica how to say, 'Peter Piper picked a peck of pickled peppercorns.'

Elica, in turn, taught Jessica and Renko the Romanian tongue-twister *'douãsprezece cocostîrci pe casa lui Cogãl-niceanu'*. 'This is meaning "twelve stork-birds on Mr Cogãl-niceanu's house".'

When it was time to leave, Jessica came to the front door to say goodbye. Elica took both of her hands and said, 'Tonight we are very, very good friends, yes?'

Jessica nodded. 'I'll see you tomorrow in school.'

Renko had buttoned his windbreaker up all wrong. Jessica unfastened it and put it straight. Renko said, 'Thanks,' and then he kissed her on the lips. 'You know something? I've had a really cool time.'

Jessica blushed; she didn't know what to say. As Renko followed Elica and Grandpa Willy down the driveway, he turned and gave her a grin. Now she understood why he had decided to stand up for her against Sue-Anne. He liked her. In fact, he really liked her. Maybe that was why he had been so aggressive toward her before. He hadn't wanted to show anybody that he found her attractive.

She had never had a boyfriend before. She didn't exactly have one now, but Renko had kissed her, hadn't he? – and not just on the cheek. She closed the door and went back toward the stairs, feeling as if she were walking on spongecake. Grannie said, 'Jessica? Are you OK, sweetie-pie? You look a little hectic.'

'No, no. I feel great. Thanks for having my friends around.'

'I feel so sorry for that little Elica.'

'Why? She's fine.'

'Don't you think it's terrible, having her father locked up in an asylum?'

'No, Grannie, he's not in a mental asylum. He's trying to get *political* asylum. Their whole family was persecuted in Romania because they were gipsies.'

'Oh,' blinked Grannie. 'She doesn't look very much like a gipsy.'

'Her family used to live in Transylvania. You know, where Dracula came from.'

'I don't know,' said Grannie, shaking her head. 'Now we're having vampires around for supper.'

When Grandpa Willy had driven Renko and Elica home, he came up to Jessica's bedroom and said, 'You've made yourself a couple of real good friends there. I'm pleased about that.'

He sat on the side of her bed and held her hand. The clock in the hallway chimed once, and he checked his wristwatch and said, 'Ten thirty already. School again tomorrow. How was it, going back today?'

'It was better,' said Jessica.

'No more of that bullying, then?'

'What bullying?' she asked, but again she couldn't stop herself from blushing.

'Come on, Jessica, Renko told me. He said that some of your classmates have been giving you a real difficult time. You should have told me, you know. I could have gone to the school and knocked some heads together.'

'I didn't like to. I thought it would only make it worse.

Besides, what with your heart and everything, I didn't want
to stress you out.'

'Sweetheart, I'm an old man now, and I'd be lying to you
if I said I was in peak condition, but since you lost your mom
and dad it's up to me to take care of you, no matter what the
stresses and strains. It's my job.'

'I'm sorry.'

'Hey, come on, you don't have to be sorry. Your granny
and me, we both love you to pieces. And Renko promised
that he's going to take care of you when you're at school.
He's a good boy, that one.'

Grandpa Willy kissed her on the forehead and then he
left, but he left the door open a few inches like he always
did. She lay back on her pillow and heard him shuffle his
way downstairs.

Then, 'Your hot chocolate's cold now, where have you
been?'

'Tucking in Jessica.'

'She's nearly seventeen, she doesn't need tucking in!
Your hot chocolate's cold!'

'I didn't even ask you for any hot chocolate.'

'That's fine! Don't worry about it! I'll pour it down
the sink!'

'Did you hear me say I wanted hot chocolate?'

'You always have hot chocolate!'

And so on, and so on. They were still bickering an hour
later, when Jessica began to close her eyes.

A breeze blew across her face, very softly at first, and then
more stiffly. At last she sat up in bed, looked around her
and realized that the breeze was coming out of the wall. She
raised her hand and she could feel it. She could even smell
it, too. It smelled of flowers, and grass, and distant rain.

'Please, help us,' whispered a voice, and she could almost
feel the breath against her ear.

Jessica closed her eyes. She hesitated for a moment and then she spoke quite loudly. 'I don't know how to help you. You'll have to tell me.'

'It's easy. Come and save us. It will take us, if you don't.'

'What is it?'

'The Stain . . . it's going to take us all.'

'The Stain? What's that?'

'Come find us, we're begging you . . . Come and save us . . .'

Jessica opened her eyes. The wallpaper was glowing, as if there was a dim light shining behind it, and the roses, irises and blessed thistles were all in silhouette. She pushed back her comforter and knelt close to the wall. The breeze made her long dark hair fly up.

'This is a dream,' she said.

But the voice whispered, 'There are no dreams, Jessica. Only different places to be.'

She stood up, balancing herself on her bed. The light from the wallpaper grew brighter and brighter, until it was so intense that she had to shield her eyes with her hand. She took one unsteady step forward, and then another. She reached the wall, and it didn't feel like a wall at all, more like a stiff damp sheet on a winter washing-line. She pushed it and it gave way, just like a sheet, and then she was battling her way through it, and suddenly it fell away behind her. She was standing barefoot in a tangle of prickly briars and this-tles, in an overgrown garden, on a brilliantly sunlit day.

Above her, the sky was primrose-colored, the same as her wallpaper, and cloudless, although she could see flocks of birds wheeling in the distance. At least they looked like flocks of birds, but when they flew closer she saw that they were nothing but the blue V-shaped patterns from her bedroom carpet.

She turned. Behind her, she could still dimly distinguish

her bed, nightstand and dressing-table, but they were separated from her by a patterned screen of flowers: all the roses and irises and blessed thistles, but plain white, because she was seeing them from the other side, their unprinted side.

'You have to help us,' whispered the voice, as if it were concerned that she might turn back.

'I will if I can,' said Jessica. 'But I can't see you. I don't know who you are.'

'Follow the flowers.'

'What?'

'Follow the flowers, and you can find us.'

'What flowers?'

Through the tangled garden, with the stilted gait of praying mantises, came seven or eight roses. They approached Jessica and stood around her, with spindly arms and legs and thorny claws. It was their faces that frightened her the most, however. The folds of their petals had taken the shape of vindictive little eyes and tight, disapproving mouths. For all of their beauty as flowers, their expressions were mean and threatening.

'This is a dream,' she repeated, although she didn't think she sounded very convincing.

One of the roses came closer than the rest, and stood with its face ruffled in the breeze. 'Have you ever suffered pain?' it asked her. Its voice was extraordinary – thin and fluting, but horribly suggestive too, as if it would really enjoy seeing her hurt.

'I hurt my foot once,' she said, lifting it up a little so that the rose could see her scars.

'You think that was painful? Has anything really awful ever gnawed at you in the night? Has anything ever come surging up from the bottom of your bed like a Great White shark and seized you in its teeth, right up to your waist? Have you ever felt the skin being torn off your ribs, and your nerves being stripped bare, and your lungs collapsing?'

'I don't know what you're talking about.'

'Oh, but you will,' said the rose. 'I'm talking about the Stain. I'm talking about the most terrible thing that lives in this world or any other world. I'm talking about something that will make your heart stop just to look at it. Do we frighten you? A few flowers out of your nightmares? You wait till you see the Stain.'

'That's if she ever does,' put in one of the meaner-looking roses. 'It's a long path and it's a very difficult path, and it's terribly easy to lose your way.'

'Who am I supposed to be saving?' asked Jessica. 'I can't save anybody if I don't even know who they are.'

'You mean you want to go back?'

'I didn't say that. I mean I want to know who's been calling for help, and why, and where they are.'

'Their names are written.'

'What do you mean? Their names are written where?'

The rose could scarcely conceal its thorny contempt. 'Where do you think? Where the gray woman in the green cloak stands and weeps.'

'And where's that?'

'Please!' whispered a voice. 'There isn't much time. Please.'

'Are you coming?' demanded the rose.

Jessica glanced back at the gloomy outline of her bedroom. High above her head, a thin swirl of clouds had formed, in the same pattern as her curtains; and the V-shaped birds were flying across it as if they were migrating far away, to somewhere sane.

This is complete and utter madness, she thought. Talk about people who need locking up in asylums. But the roses started to mantis-walk away from her, with an irritating claw-like rustle, and after only a moment's hesitation she went after them.

Through the Woods

The roses led her down a wide, windy hill. At first she thought that they were walking through dry, knee-high grass, scattered with brown poppies; but when she looked down she realized that it was the pattern from the cover that she had stuck on her geography workbook.

Not only was the sky growing darker, but the wind was rising, so that Jessica's sleep-T billowed and leaves came whirling through the air, as well as fragments of all kinds of decorations and patterns. She saw the curlicues from her grandmother's lacy tablecloth, and the leaves and stars that were embossed around the edge of Grandpa Willy's leather-topped desk. She saw spots and dots and feathers and flowers, and even the horseshoes, clubs and four-leaf clovers from the Lucky Charms cereal box.

'Hurry!' demanded the roses. 'We don't have all day!'

They reached the foot of the hill and began to make their way down a narrow, winding gully. The grass from Jessica's geography book lashed at their ankles. The wind had lifted to a soft, morbid scream, and it was filled with a blizzard of carpet patterns, dress designs and fragments of curtain material. Jessica was lashed on the cheek by a bramble from the wallpaper in Grannie's sewing-room. She lost her balance, stumbled, and fell down on one knee, but the roses came ripping back and shrieked at her, 'Up! Up! We haven't far to go, and it's much too dangerous!'

This is a dream, Jessica tried to persuade herself, but now

she was quite sure that it wasn't a dream at all, that she was living every moment of it, and it was real. No matter how hard she tried to wake up, she was still slithering down the gully with the roses and she knew that there was only one way for her to get back to her bedroom, and that was to turn around and run there, on her own.

As they neared the foot of the gully they began to run into gorse bushes and scrub, which snagged at Jessica's T-shirt and caught in her hair. The gorse grew thicker and higher, and soon they were entering a gloomy wood filled with hundreds of slender trees with shining dark-brown trunks and curled-up branches – except that they weren't trees at all, but hat-stands, and what had seemed at first sight to be overshadowing foliage was thousands of hats, both men's and women's, trilbies and fedoras and black funeral hats with ostrich feathers.

'Faster,' insisted the roses.

It was so shadowy in the woods that Jessica could only just make out their spindly arms and legs, and underneath the heaps of overhanging hats the air was suffocating, like hiding in a closet filled with your grandparents' old clothes, wishing that your party guests would hurry up and find you.

They emerged at last on the banks of a wide, iridescent river. The light was failing fast, and Jessica began to realize that the hours behind the wall seemed to pass much more urgently, as if time itself were in a panic.

The river was fifty or sixty feet wide, and the water wasn't water but rippling moiré silk of the iciest blue. On the far side stood a landing-stage constructed of yellow majolica tiles, and behind the landing-stage rose trees so dark that they almost looked black – yet sparkling, all of them, with millions and millions of tiny lights. They reminded her of the trees she had seen in her fairy books, Arthur Rackham trees with twisted trunks and hollows where hobgoblins secreted themselves, and whose upper branches were clouded with fairies.

Already the day had grown so dusky that it was a moment or two before Jessica realized that somebody was standing on the landing-stage. It was a child, a girl of nine or ten, wearing a simple white nightgown with long sleeves, and a white surgical mask that completely covered her nose and mouth. She stood looking at Jessica across the endlessly rippling river, her hair occasionally lifted by the evening wind. She was juggling five differently colored balls, quite nonchalantly, as if she had been juggling all her life.

'You came,' she whispered, and even though she was so far away Jessica could hear her quite distinctly, almost as if she were right inside her head.

'Who are you?' Jessica called out. 'What do you want me to do?'

'I'm Phoebe. I'm supposed to be the naughty one. I'm the one who teased the cat. I'm the one who spooned the strawberry jelly into Uncle Richard's hat.'

'I still don't understand.'

'You have to find the Stain. You have to wash it away forever.'

'I don't know where it is. I don't even know *what* it is.'

'It's growing and it's spreading and soon it's going to catch us. Three days and three nights, tickety-tock, that's all we have left.'

'Where do I look for it? I just don't know what you want me to do!'

Behind the girl, the sparkling in the fairy-trees grew more intense, and Jessica saw wisps of smoke. The trees weren't sparkling with fairies, they were actually on fire. She could smell burning on the wind, and hear the popping of twigs.

'I have to go,' said the girl. 'Please look for the Stain. Please, or it's going to take us all, forever. No more juggling. No more games.' Suddenly, she tossed all of her juggling-balls into the air and they weren't juggling-balls at all but brightly colored spots from the laundry-room wallpaper, and they were blown away into the wind and out of sight.

'When will I see you again?' asked Jessica.

'Meet me tomorrow by the sea.'

'Where's that? How do I get there?'

'The roses will show you . . . Now, I have to go. No more time for pepper in the sugar bowl. No more apple-pie beds. No more childhood, not for us.'

Jessica turned around to talk to the roses, but they had all hurried away into the gathering shadows; and when she looked back across the river Phoebe had disappeared too, and the yellow-tiled landing-stage was empty. Jessica was alone on the riverbank in the strangest of worlds, with dark falling fast and the wind howling even more eerily, as if it wasn't a wind at all but the sobbing of people in serious pain.

She left the river behind her and began to climb back uphill, into the stuffy hat-covered forest. It was even gloomier than it had been just a few minutes before, and even more suffocating, and she prayed that she wouldn't get lost. What would happen if you went into the wall and couldn't find out how to get back again? Nobody would ever know you were there, and they would never think of sending a search party into your wallpaper to find you, would they? She tried to keep herself calm, but she began to limp faster, almost breaking into a run, anxious to get out of the woods and back to the top of the hill before it grew totally dark.

At last, panting, she saw the faint violet light of the evening sky through the hat-stands. She slowed down a little, because now she was sure that she was going the right way. As she did so, however, she thought she heard a crackling noise quite close behind her, and off to her left. Probably those horrible roses, following her and trying to frighten her. But then she heard another crackle, and a complicated splintering, and this was far too loud to be a few malevolent flowers.

She stopped, and listened. She still could hear the river, but only faintly now, and every now and then the soft dropping sound of a fallen hat. More than anything else, she could hear her own blood rushing in her ears, *whoosh, whoosh, whoosh.*

It's the roses, she thought. It's the roses, because they're mean and they're spiteful and they know that I can't run very fast because of my limp. She continued to walk toward the treeline, feeling irritated rather than scared, but then she heard a *crackle-crackle-crackle* and she could sense that something really big was rushing up behind her and she turned, and screamed. A huge jagged shape was running toward her, making a noise like chairs and tables being smashed up with half a dozen axes. She saw four blazing red eyes and two stretched-open mouths, and rows and rows of sharply pointed teeth. The thing let out a deafening roar and it was only because she tripped and fell over sideways that it missed her. All the same, one of its claws caught against the sleeve of her sleep-T and ripped it.

She found herself on all fours, scrambling across the forest floor, her hands and knees prickled not by pine needles but by thousands of glittering hatpins. With a harsh growl, the thing came running back around the hat-stands, and now Jessica could begin to see what it was: a wolf-like creature, except that it wasn't made of flesh and blood, but varnished wood, broken into sharp pointed pieces, with splinters instead of fur. It had two faces, one the right way up and the other, immediately below it, upside-down. Four eyes, two muzzles, two mouths crammed with teeth. It was the walnut veneer on her closet, come to life. It had two faces because the door panel had been made from the same section of wood, cut in half and fitted with one half facing up and the matching piece facing down.

It had always frightened her, especially at night when she was lying in bed, trying to sleep. It seemed to stare at her with all four eyes as if it had only one purpose in life and that was to eat her. But here, in the woods, circling toward her, making that crackling noise with every step, it was so terrifying that she couldn't stop herself from whimpering.

She managed to stand up, balancing herself against one of the hat-stands. The wooden wolf lowered its head and growled at her with both of its mouths. It had charged at her wildly before, but now it had obviously realized how weak she was, and how scared, and it walked toward her slowly, one seven-clawed paw in front of the other, as if it were relishing the smell of her fear with each of its four flared nostrils.

Jessica backed away, reaching out blindly for the hat-stand right behind her. Six or seven hats dropped onto the forest floor – a black silk opera hat, a priest's biretta, a huge Edwardian confection of black eagle's feathers; then a sudden tumble of trilbies and a deerstalker. The wooden wolf kept on coming after her, every sinew of its body creaking and squeaking.

Oh please God don't let it hurt me, Jessica prayed. If it's going to kill me, please let it kill me quickly. She knew enough about pain from the time when she was recovering from her parents' car crash. The kind of pain that the roses had been talking about: the pain that made you feel as if something was eating you alive.

Now the wooden wolf was only a few paces away. It could have easily sprung at her and knocked her down with one jump, but she could hear it breathing her in, breathing her in. It must have been waiting for this moment for over a year – ever since it had first seen her enter her bedroom and stared at her, mute but hungry, from her closet door.

She stumbled backward, and the next hat-stand swayed, so that more hats fell down. She took hold of the hat-stand and swung it around so that it toppled over. It fell against another hat-stand, and that in turn knocked another one over. Jessica limped back faster and faster, knocking over every hat-stand she came to. It started a chain reaction all the way through the forest, until hat-stands were clattering down everywhere and thousands of hats were pattering onto the ground like soft applause.

The wooden wolf managed to jump over the first few tangles of hat-stands, but as Jessica pushed more and more of them over, they formed a criss-cross barrier that stopped it in its tracks. It roared at her in fury and frustration, and began to circle quickly around to the left, so that it could outflank her, but she ducked down onto her hands and knees and crawled underneath a tunnel of fallen hat-stands until she was only a few metres away from the edge of the forest. She had hatpins sticking in her hands and knees, but she didn't care. The wooden wolf was still running around the heaps of hats, hungry for her flesh and thirsty for her blood.

She reached the gorse bushes and began to limp uphill. It was night-time now, and up above the windy hilltop she could see millions and millions of stars, all forming the pattern of Grannie's best lace curtains. She quickly turned her head to see if the wooden wolf were still coming after her, but between the gorse bushes it was too dark for her to see. She kept limping upward, gasping for breath, and trying not to think of the lines she had learned at school: 'Like one that on a lonesome road/doth walk in fear and dread/because he knows a fearful fiend doth close behind him tread.'

She crested the hill, and now – no more than a hundred metres away – she could make out the tangled garden where she had first entered the wall. But as she started on the last stretch, hobbling through the dry grass from her geography book, she heard the clattering of claws up the gully behind her and they were coming very, very fast. She turned to look, even though she didn't really want to, and just as she did, the wooden wolf appeared, its four eyes burning like the narrow grilles in a hot coke furnace, its lips drawn back to reveal crowds of broken and ragged teeth.

Then – worse – Jessica heard an answering snarl from not far off to her right, and more sharp crackling noises. At first she couldn't see what it was, but then she glimpsed the gleam of varnished wood in the darkness. Another wooden wolf was coming after her, and she realized that, no matter how much she hurried, she wasn't going to be able to reach the garden before at least one of the wolves was upon her.

Into the Light

S he tried to run faster, but her ankle was so weak that she kept twisting it and falling onto her knees. Again and again she managed to pick herself up and keep on hobbling forward, but now the first wooden wolf was only a few bounds behind her and she knew with a rising feeling of desperation that she couldn't escape it. Its voracious breathing sounded like somebody sawing furiously at a table leg, and she could almost feel its teeth tearing into her back muscles.

Out of the corner of her eye she could see the second wooden wolf already keeping pace with her, still fifteen or twenty metres away but gaining on her all the time.

She wrenched her ankle yet again, really badly this time, and fell sideways. She tried to crawl away but it was no use. The first wolf came circling around her, panting, and the second wolf quickly came up to join it.

'You're not real!' Jessica shouted at them, almost screaming. 'You're part of my dream, that's all! You're doors! You're nothing but doors! You can't be wolves!'

But she knew it was futile. She had never had a dream in which she could feel the wind in her face, and the grass under her knees, and such an agonizing pain in her ankle.

The wooden wolves creaked closer and closer. They were so near now that she could even smell their breath: vinegary, like the inside of old cupboards.

'Don't hurt me,' she begged. 'Please don't hurt me.' But

how could a wolf understand what she was saying, let alone a wolf made out of nothing but splintered wood?

Just as she thought the wooden wolves were going to jump on her, though, the fields all around them were abruptly lit up by a blinding white light. It was still night, but the grass all around her was illuminated as bright as day. The wooden wolves swiveled their hideous heads around, this way and that, and one of them started to back away nervously.

Jessica shielded her eyes with her hand. Peering between her fingers, she saw what looked like a thousand-watt electric lightbulb slowly bobbing its way toward her. The wooden wolves obviously found it frightening, because the second one backed away too, and then both of them turned and crackled off toward the brow of the hill. In only a few moments they had disappeared.

The dazzling light came nearer, and when Jessica tried to look at it she saw dozens of green blobs floating in front of her eyes. It stopped only a few feet away, wavering slightly.

'You can get up now,' said a voice. 'They've gone now, and they won't dare to come back for you while I'm here.' The voice was high-pitched, with a metallic, pinging quality to it, more like a music box than a voice.

Jessica slowly lowered her hand, although she still had to keep her eyes squinted against the brilliance. Gradually she began to make out what the light was. A slender, transparent creature that floated in the air – a creature made of glass, with crystal wings and a shining glass globe for a head. Inside the globe, Jessica could see a face that was formed out of filaments of pure light – sly, elfin eyes, a spiky nose, and a mouth that was pursed up in self-satisfaction and amusement.

'What are you?' asked Jessica.

'You're the one who's supposed to know all about fairies,' the creature retorted.

'You can't be a fairy. There are no such things.'

'There are no such things as wolves made out of closet doors, either; or trees that grow hats; or rivers made of silk.'

'There are. I've seen them.'

'Seen them or dreamed them?'

'This isn't a dream. This is real.'

'If this is real, then I'm a real fairy, aren't I? Fairies aren't all butterfly wings and sparkly wands and ballet skirts. Fairies come in all shapes and disguises, most of them ugly and some of them highly dangerous and all of them as spiteful as monkeys. The very word "fairy" means fate.'

As the creature spoke, another light came floating toward them across the grass, and then another, until the slope was so brightly lit that Jessica felt as if the whole world had become an over-exposed photograph.

'These are the best friends that anybody could ever have,' said the creature. 'The fairies of light and brilliance. These are the fairies who illuminate your room at night and turn the monsters back into bathrobes and the skulls back into table lamps. Without them, the darkness would be swarming with all kinds of demons and misshapen creatures. But they keep their distance, mostly, because they fear reality, you see, and truth; and most of all they fear being seen for what they really are.'

The light-fairies clustered around Jessica and escorted her slowly down the slope, not hurrying her, treating her almost as if she were royal, or very precious to them anyway, dipping and curtseying as they went.

'You're safe now,' said the creature as they crossed the overgrown garden and reached the pattern of Jessica's bedroom wallpaper.

'I have to come back,' said Jessica. 'I know it's asking a lot, but will you help me again, if I do?'

'Oh no, you shouldn't come back. Stay on your own side of the wall, where it's safer.'

'But there are children here who need me to save them. They've been begging me.'

'There are many people here who beg for this and beg for that. Some beg for chocolate cake, or puppies. Some beg to differ, and some beg to die.'

'But the girl I saw – Phoebe – she wants me to come back and rescue her. She said that something called the Stain is coming to get her.'

'The Stain will get us all in the end. There's nothing that one lame girl can do about it. Fate, remember!'

'What is it, the Stain?'

'The Stain is what makes the world frightening and the dark dark. The Stain is all the horror you could ever think of, and even more horror that you couldn't. The very best thing that you can do now is forget all about Phoebe and everything you've seen on this side of the wall, and go back to where it's cozy, and if you ever think about what you saw here, persuade yourself that you once had a nightmare, and this was it.'

'I can't leave those children. They're so scared.'

'Of course they're scared. They have every reason to be. And you have every reason not to return.'

Jessica looked back toward the brow of the faraway hill. It was already beginning to grow light, and she could see the silhouettes of storks flying high above the trees, except the storks were the patterns on her grandmother's spoon handles, and the trees were the lace curtains halfway down the stairs.

The light-fairies were gradually dimming, and one by one they switched themselves off, leaving only the first one, who had saved her from the wooden wolves. There was a smell of burning leaves in the air, and somebody in the distance was playing a whistle, the kind of regretful lament that makes you stop, and listen, and wonder why you feel so sad.

'Don't come back,' said the creature gently. 'Some people are destined for some worlds, and others are destined for different worlds altogether. This world – this isn't yours.'

Jessica reached out to touch the creature, but its glass head was much too hot, like a real lightbulb. 'Thank you,' she said. 'I don't know what would have happened to me if you hadn't chased those wolves away.'

'Better not to think about it. Blood, you know; and having your lunchpipes torn out.'

Jessica turned to face the wallpaper pattern. But she hesitated and said, 'Supposing I can't get through? What then?'

'Oh, you can get through,' the creature reassured her. 'You are one of those who will always get through.'

Jessica closed her eyes, took a deep breath and stepped smartly forward. Just as before, she felt for one panicky moment as if she were battling her way through a sheet hanging on a washing-line. For a few suffocating seconds she was all tangled up, and then suddenly she was clear of it, and standing on the rug in the middle of her bedroom.

Her bed lay cold, with the sheets twisted up just as she had left them. The sun was already gleaming behind the trees, and the house was beginning to fill with light. For a split second she thought she could still hear somebody playing a whistle, very far away, but then the music was gone, and there was silence.

She crossed over to her dressing-table. The girl in the mirror stared back at her very solemnly. 'I went through the wall,' said the girl in the mirror. 'I went through the wall and I met roses that talked to me and wolves made of wood.'

As soon as she said that, she whipped around and looked anxiously at her closet, with its walnut veneer. The wolf

faces were still there, but smooth and varnished, and showing no sign of sudden life. All the same, she didn't attempt to
touch them, and in the morning when she opened the closet
doors to get her clothes out she snatched at the handles very
quickly, and stepped well back.

She met Renko and Elica by the lockers at school. Sue-Anne
was there too, chattering to her friends, and she made a
point of turning her back when Jessica arrived. She sniffed
loudly, although she didn't dare say anything because Renko
was there.

Elica was wearing a colorful scarf on her head so that
she actually looked like a gipsy. Renko had his favorite
sweatshirt on, emblazoned with the colors of the Connecticut
Huskies. His hair was sticking up as if he hadn't combed it
since he got out of bed, but Jessica thought that made him
look cute, rather than scruffy.

'I went through!' she said, quietly but excitedly.

'You went through what?' frowned Renko.

'The wallpaper. I stood on my bed and walked right
through.'

Renko looked at Elica and Elica looked back at Renko.

'You went through the wallpaper? Like, to where? Solid-
brick Land?'

'You have dream,' Elica suggested. 'You want this so
much lot, you have dream you go.'

'Elica, I was wide awake. I went through and there's
a whole world in there. It's like . . . Patternworld. Everything's made out of patterns from the real world. The grass,
the trees, the birds, the sky, everything. Look – see this –'
she took her geography workbook out of her locker and
held it up in front of them – 'this paper has a grass pattern
on it, right?, with poppies. Last night I walked through
this grass. I walked through this grass until I came to the
edge of the book and then I went down a hill and—'

95

Renko was staring at her very seriously with his pale-gray eyes. 'Jessica,' he said.

'What? You don't believe me? Renko, I swear to you. I swear on the Holy Bible I went there. I went through. You heard those children calling for help. I saw one of them. I actually saw her. She was down by this river and she said her name was Phoebe. Only these wolves came after me and I had to run.'

'Wolves?'

'Well, not real wolves. Wooden wolves, from my closet doors.'

Renko slowly shook his head. 'Come on, Jessica. Maybe the Sheriff was right. Maybe that blow on the nut . . . Look, I'm not saying you don't, like, genuinely believe this stuff, but nobody can walk through wallpaper, and there's no world with wooden wolves in it, I promise you.'

'I have to go back. The Stain's coming to take those children, and if I don't save them then nobody will.'

'Jessica, have you heard yourself?'

Jessica suddenly found that her eyes were filling up with tears. 'I thought you believed me. You heard those children yourself.'

'Hearing some kids' voices down a chimney isn't the same thing as walking through a solid wall.'

'You don't cry, Jessica,' said Elica. 'You have a dream of this place, so what? Is bad? This is good to dream of other place. Like my father dream of America and always say, one day I will take you to this place with happy people and kindness and golden arches.'

Jessica wiped her eyes with a tissue and blew her nose. 'I'm sorry . . . I didn't sleep very much, that's all. But I was there, Renko, I absolutely promise you. Look,' she showed the pinprick marks in her hands that the hatpins had made, marks she had taken care to conceal from Grannie at breakfast.

'OK, OK,' said Renko, and put his arm around her shoulder – a gesture which didn't go unnoticed by Sue-Anne, who gave a dismissive toss of her curls and said, 'No taste, some people!'

They left the lockers and started to walk along the corridor to their English class. Jessica said, 'Listen . . . how about sleeping over tonight?'

'What?'

'If you both sleep over, I can prove it to you. I can actually take you there.'

Renko stopped. 'You're really serious about this, aren't you?'

'Well, let's put it this way: if it's real, I want you to see it. But if it's only that knock on the head, giving me delusions, then I want to know about that, too, so that I can go to the doctor.'

'I don't know,' said Renko. 'Anyway, won't your grandmother worry about – you know . . . ?'

'Please,' Jessica begged him. 'What have you got to lose?'

Down By the Sea

G rannie apologized because she hadn't been expecting visitors and she had only corned-beef hash for supper. Renko didn't seem to mind: he cleared his plate and asked for seconds.

'You're sure it's OK if Renko and Elica sleep over?' Jessica asked her as she helped Grannie to dry the dishes.

'I couldn't be more pleased, sweetheart. You don't want to be spending all of your time with old relics like us.'

'You're not relics. I love you, both of you.'

'All the same, we're old, and you need to be mixing with young folks, with young ideas. Your Grandpa Willy thinks garage music is what they play at the filling-station. Just you be sensible.' And she gave Jessica a meaningful glance.

'Yes, Grannie,' Jessica replied.

After supper they went upstairs to Jessica's bedroom. 'I'm supposed to meet Phoebe by the ocean,' said Jessica. 'I don't know how to get there, but I guess the roses might help us, if we can find them.'

Renko sat in the swivel chair in front of Jessica's desk, swinging himself from side to side. He didn't say anything, but she could tell by the expression on his face that he still didn't believe her at all. Elica stood in front of the mirror and pinned up her hair with some of Jessica's sparkly barrettes. 'I look like princess, yes?'

'We'll have to take my flashlight, just in case the wooden wolves come after us.'

'Sure,' said Renko. 'Wouldn't like to be eaten alive by a closet door, would we?'

'Please, Renko. Don't make fun. You have to believe you can do this, otherwise you won't be able to.'

'OK, OK.' He nodded toward the wallpaper. 'What time are you planning on going?'

'As soon as my granny and grandpa have gone to bed. I don't want them coming in here and finding us gone.'

Elica said, 'You believe this so much. I don't want you to have disappointment.'

'I don't think I will, Elica. And I don't think you will either.'

They talked and played music until well after ten, when Grandpa Willy came in to wish them good-night. 'Don't stay up all night, kids. It's school in the morning, remember.'

Grannie came in behind him with milk and home-made cinnamon cookies. 'I used to love slumber parties when I was young. My mother used to make us a whole picnic, with fried chicken and jellies and everything.'

She kissed Jessica good-night and then followed Grandpa across the landing.

'Did you let the cat in?'

'I thought the darn cat was in already.'

'You know she wasn't in. You put her out yourself.'

'I know I did, but I thought you let her back in again. She never stays out long in the snow.'

'I can't trust you to do anything.'

'I can trust you, though. I can trust you to nag me into an early grave.'

Grandpa went down to let the cat in, grumbling all the way, and then he came back up again, still grumbling. At last Jessica heard their bedroom door close. She turned to

Renko and Elica and said, 'OK . . . we can go now. Are you ready for this?'

Renko approached the wall, and knocked on it. 'Seems pretty solid to me.'

'The wall is, yes. But the pattern on the wallpaper isn't.'

'Right . . . you'd better show us how it's done.'

Jessica came and stood beside him, her nose only centimeters away from the wallpaper. 'There's nothing difficult about it. All you have to do is take a breath and step forward. Like this.'

She took a single step toward the wall and felt it give way. A moment's struggling against it and she was through, standing in the overgrown garden under a pale morning sky. She turned around and she could dimly see Renko and Elica standing in her bedroom, their mouths both open in stupefaction. She could even hear them talking, although their voices were very muffled.

'Where did she go?'

'I am not knowing, Renko. She disappear like *poof* !'

Jessica went back to the wall and shouted at them. 'I'm here! I'm inside the pattern! All you have to do is take a step!'

'I can hear her,' said Renko. 'She must be there, I can hear her!' But still he wouldn't step forward.

'Come on!' Jessica shouted. 'It's easy!'

Renko didn't move and Elica even backed away a little. Exasperated, Jessica plunged her hand in between the roses and took hold of Renko's sleeve. She pulled him and, like somebody stepping through a curtained window, he appeared in the garden.

He looked around him and slowly shook his head. 'You were right. Holy Moly. I can't believe it. You can get through.'

'Now you, Elica!' called Jessica. She pushed her hand

through the wallpaper again, caught hold of Elica's arm and pulled her into the garden too.

'Is magic,' said Elica, wide-eyed. She looked back at the wallpaper and touched it, just to make sure that she was really on the other side.

'Look at these bushes,' Renko enthused. 'They're all made out of that leaf pattern on your grandma's couch. And these apples . . . I saw those same apples on the supper plates on her dresser. Only those were painted, and these are for real.'

'The flowers!' said Elica. 'All this daisy from table-cloth!'

High above their heads, swans flew that weren't swans at all, but curly moldings from the dining-room chairs; and in the distance they could see trees that were clusters of green lampshades, with fringes all around them.

'I can't believe we're here,' said Renko. 'I thought you were going bananas, I really did.'

'Maybe we are all banana,' put in Elica.

Renko picked one of the apples and bit into it. 'You're telling me I'm imagining this apple? I can feel it; I can taste it.'

But Jessica was growing anxious. 'We have to find out where the ocean is. Time passes real quick here. Like one minute it's morning and the next minute the sun's going down. At least the roses were here before, to show me the way.'

As if it had been listening to her, one of the roses appeared from underneath the overgrown bushes and stalked toward her, its mean little face uplifted.

'Is walking flower!' gasped Elica. 'Is flower with face!'

'I've seen everything now,' said Renko. 'How am I going to tell the guys at school about this? "Oh, hi, Brad, I went through the wall in Jessica's bedroom last night and met this rose-bush that walked."'

'And talked,' hissed the rose.

'Oh, yes,' said Renko, laughing in amazement. 'That would make it a whole lot more believable.'

'You came back,' the rose said to Jessica in a withering tone. 'Didn't the Light People tell you not to?'

'I have to save the children. I can't just leave them here until the Stain takes them.'

'Many people try to save their friends and their loved ones, but hardly anyone succeeds. You should go back.'

'I want to see Phoebe. She said she'd meet me beside the sea.'

'You can't save her. You can't save anybody.'

'I have to try.'

The rose turned its face so that its petals were muffled by the breeze, altering its expression, making it appear softer. 'Yes, well. I suppose you have to try. It doesn't really matter if it's impossible, does it, so long as you try?'

'Then tell me where the ocean is.'

'Out of the garden and off to the left and down the zigzag path. But don't let the darkness catch up with you, and whatever you do watch out for the robes.'

'The robes? What are the robes?'

'You'll know when you see them,' said the rose. 'And then you'll know that running's no use.'

'How much time do we have before it gets dark?' asked Renko. He was obviously embarrassed that he was talking to a flower, but there wasn't any alternative.

'As long as it takes for the light to fade away,' the rose replied unhelpfully.

'Yes, but how long is that exactly?'

'Exactly long enough for you to wish that you hadn't wasted your time asking.'

'Then we'd better go, hadn't we?'

Jessica said, 'Wait, Renko. You two don't have to come with me. If the rose is right, and it's dangerous—'

'If it's dangerous, that's all the more reason I ought to come.'

'Elica?' asked Jessica. 'How about you?'

'In Romania for gipsies there was much dangerous. We laugh at dangerous. Ha! Ha! Who cares about you, dangerous? I will come too.'

'All right, then. You've got the flashlight, haven't you, in case we meet any of those wooden wolves?'

'Least of your problems, wooden wolves,' said the rose sniffily.

They left the garden and started to walk up a long diagonal slope. The ground was thick with tiny purple-and-white flowers, which Jessica recognized as one of the diamond patches on her grandmother's quilt. By the time they reached the top of the slope they could already smell the sea, and they could see a thin glitter on the horizon, underneath a cloudbank of embroidered cushions.

Twenty or thirty metres below the crest of the slope stood a wooden gate with an arch over the top of it – the same gate that appeared in the stained-glass windows in the kitchen. Beyond the gate ran a zigzag path, making its way between the trees, over a small green hill and round a cottage with white-painted walls and smoke looping out of its chimney.

The air was noticeably chillier than it had been when they first arrived in the overgrown garden, and Jessica noticed that the sun had already moved halfway around the sky. She thought for a moment that she could hear that sad fluting music again, but the breeze made a ruffling sound in her ears and she couldn't be sure.

There was no need for them to open the gate because it stood on its own in the middle of the slope. 'Pretty useless kind of gate,' said Renko. 'Like having a front door with no house.' But Jessica was reminded of what Mrs Crawford had told her, about the door standing alone in the desert.

They walked around the gate and kept on going until they

103

reached the zigzag path. It was made of knobbly yellow glass, exactly like the path that appeared in the kitchen window. How many times Jessica had imagined walking along it, between the trees and over the little hill, and now she actually was. For some reason it made her feel regretful, as if she had lost something by walking along it in real life. She had lost the dream that she had always had about it when she was little, when her father and mother were still alive. In those days it had seemed like a comforting imaginary world to which she could escape when she felt unhappy. Now it was leading her who knew where.

Elica sang a gipsy song as they walked, about a man who made himself a wife out of old clothes and straw, and when he kissed her she came to life. The wind blew stronger and stronger, and paper seagulls wheeled over their heads. They reached the white cottage. It had a small front garden crowded with brightly colored glass flowers that tinkled like wind-chimes, ruby-reds and sapphires and purples. Its windows were made of opaque yellow glass out of which a warm light shone, as if everybody inside the cottage was cozy and safe.

'Maybe we should see if there's anyone home,' Renko suggested.

But Jessica could see that they didn't have long before it grew dark. 'No . . . we'd better keep moving. I don't know what the robes are, but I didn't like the sound of them at all.'

Running From the Robes

They walked through a copse of tall blue stylized trees from the living-room curtains, and then they found themselves on the seashore. The beach was wide and flat, so that there were scarcely any waves, and in the distance the ocean glittered the palest green. Elica shivered and said, 'Is cold here. Where is this girl?'

'There,' said Jessica, and pointed. About a hundred meters away, five dining-room chairs were arranged on the sand. In one of the chairs sat Phoebe, still wearing a long white nightgown and a white cotton face-mask, and swinging one leg. The other four chairs were empty.

It seemed to take them forever to cross the beach. All the time the sun kept edging further and further down toward the horizon, and their shadows grew longer and longer, with wide ankles and tiny heads. At last they reached the chairs and Phoebe looked up at them, shading her eyes with her hand. With her face-mask it was impossible to see what she looked like, but she had long shiny blond hair and wide brown eyes with plum-colored circles underneath them, and where the wind blew her nightdress against her they could see that she was pitifully thin.

'You came,' she said in a muffled voice. 'I didn't think you would.'

'I want to help you, that's why. These are my friends Renko and Elica. They want to help you too.'

Phoebe stared at the visitors' brightly colored clothes for

105

a moment. 'We only have two days and two nights left. Tickety-tock, tickety-tock. Then the Stain will be coming to take us.'

'"Us"?' said Renko. 'Where are the rest of you?'

'They're not very well. None of us is very well.' She gave a hard little cough, as if she were straining to prove it.

'What's the matter with you?'

'Spotted fever. I was the last one to catch it, so I'm not so bad. But the others are pretty sick.'

'Spotted fever?' said Renko. 'I never heard of it.'

'A lot of children in Litchfield County caught it. Three of my schoolfriends died.' Phoebe coughed again, and this time she went on coughing and coughing until Jessica thought that she would never stop. 'We've been sick like this for as long as I can remember. If you can't find a way to wash away the Stain, and it comes to take us, at least we won't be sick anymore.'

'How did you get here?' asked Jessica.

'Our mother and father brought us here, when we first caught the fever. They said we had to stay here or else we were all going to die. They kept on bringing us different medicines, but all of the medicines tasted horrible and none of them worked, and then one day our mother and father stopped coming.'

'How long ago was that?'

Phoebe kept on swinging her leg. 'I don't know . . . time is kind of different here. Not long ago, but ages and ages.'

'How come you've only got two days and two nights left?'

'That's what the Light People told us. Did you meet the Light People?'

'Yes, I did. They saved me from the wooden wolves.'

'The Light People say that good times always pass quickly; bad times always go extra-slow. A happy year can feel like it's all over in a week; but the Stain is so evil that it takes fifty-two years before it leaks out. One year for every week.'

'But now it's going to leak out?'

'At seven minutes past eleven tomorrow evening. That's what the Light People told me.'

'Can't you just come with us?' asked Renko. 'We can take you to a doctor as soon as you get back through the wall.'

'Our mother told us not to go back until she brought us a cure. She hasn't come, so there can't be a cure. You don't think she would have left us here if there was, do you?'

'Wait,' said Jessica. 'If we've never even heard of spotted fever, then maybe there is a cure. I mean, maybe they found a way to wipe it out years ago. Maybe your mother stopped coming because, well – maybe she just couldn't, for some reason.' She didn't want to say 'maybe she died', but it was hard to think of any other explanation. Days went by so quickly in this world behind the wallpaper that it was quite possible that Phoebe and her brothers and sisters had been here for years.

'We go back to find out what is spotted fever,' Elica suggested. 'Then we come back, give you medicine.'

'I think that's all we can do,' Renko agreed. 'But if this Stain thing is going to take them tomorrow, we'd better do it quick.'

It was almost dark now, and the wind was blowing even colder. On the horizon, Jessica could see a ship with black sails, and even though it must have been miles away she could hear its timbers creaking and the sinister rumble of its canvas. In the real world, the ship was embossed on the metal coal scuttle in her grandparents' living-room, but here it was a pirate galleon with a crew that could only be guessed at. She said to Phoebe, 'Will you be all right until tomorrow? I'll talk to Dr Leeming and see what we can do to help you. I promise you, Phoebe, we'll do everything we can to save you.'

The tide was sliding in, and the water began to wash against the legs of Phoebe's chair. She kept on swinging her leg, swinging her leg, so that her toes went *splish, splash, splish, splash*. Renko took hold of Jessica's hand and said, 'Come on, I think we'd better get back. There's nothing else we can do tonight.'

They left Phoebe on the beach and walked back the way they had come. By the time they had reached the blue stylized trees it was very dark, and even though they had Jessica's flashlight to guide them they stumbled several times. There were no lights shining in the cottage windows, because of course it was only a window made of stained glass and the sun had set.

As they neared the end of the zigzag path, Jessica thought she could hear a rushing sound, like scores of people running through the bushes. The sound was coming toward them, louder and louder, and it was coming very quickly.

'Stop!' she warned. 'Renko, Elica – can you hear that?'

They stopped and listened. 'Sounds like somebody's in a hurry,' said Renko.

'Who can it be?' asked Elica in alarm.

Jessica shone her flashlight up ahead of them. At first she couldn't see anything except the trees and bushes and the gleaming glass surface of the zigzag path. But suddenly she saw something bobbing, and then another, and then another, and before she could cry out a warning more than a score of dark shapes came running at them out of the darkness.

She recognized at once what they were, and so did Renko and Elica. Every child would have recognized them from those fear-filled nights when the wind sucks under the bedroom door like a hungry monster and the morning seems like a hundred years away. 'The robes,' said Renko, and his voice was filled with such dread that Jessica instinctively started to run.

They all ran. And behind them, close on their heels, came all the grotesque creatures that take shape at night from robes that hang on bedroom doors, or clothes that are carelessly tossed over the backs of chairs. Some of them were headless, but others had hoods that contained nothing but darkness, or hideous faces that were formed from crumpled cloth. As they came closer they began to howl and scream, and Elica screamed too, out of sheer terror.

When you see them, the rose had warned them, you'll know that running's no use. And it wasn't, because the robes ran so fast, their sleeves waving, and as they ran they made a loud flurrying sound, like a hundred blankets being furiously shaken out.

Jessica, limping, started to fall behind. Renko grabbed hold of her hand and pulled her along faster. 'Don't look back!' he panted. The robes were only a few feet behind them now, and their howling was even more blood-curdling.

They ran past the darkened cottage, and there stood the gate. 'Through here!' Jessica gasped.

'Go around it, we don't have time!'

'No! Through here!' Jessica insisted.

They reached the gate. It had a rusted metal catch and Renko had to knock it with his fist to try and open it. At that moment, in a hideous rush, the robes caught up with them. A hooded robe seized Jessica by the shoulder, and even though its arm was only toweling she could feel its long bony claws through the fabric. She tried to pull herself free, but it caught hold of her with its other claw and twisted her around.

'Get off me!' she screamed. 'Get off me!'

The robe was tall, much taller than she was. It towered over her, its hood raised, and inside the darkness of its hood she could just make out the glitter of agate-yellow eyes, and the gleaming of shark-like teeth. Its claws wrenched at her T-shirt and scratched at her arms.

Elica was screaming too. A hunched-up beast that looked like a black jacket had pulled her to the ground, while five or six other robes clustered greedily around her. She kicked at it but it caught her ankle and held onto it, and began to pull her toward its gaping zipper.

'No!' cried Elica, in panic. 'No! If you hurt me, my father kill you!'

The jacket dragged her closer, its sleeves flailing like a beached walrus. Inside its leathery body cavity crawled masses of spiders and beetles, thousands of them. They even dropped out of its sleeves into Elica's hair. She thrashed and struggled, but the jacket was far too strong for her. It was invested, like all of the robes, with the terrible power of nightmares.

Renko tried to wrench away the robe that was tearing at Jessica, but the creature knocked him away with a single thunderous flap of its sleeve. He got up again, winded, and came back to try again, but Jessica shouted at him, 'Open the gate! Renko – open the gate!'

Renko hesitated, unsure of what he should really do, but again Jessica shrilled, 'Open it!' and he turned around and gave it a kick. It didn't budge. He kicked it again, and again. Elica was screaming and spitting at the same time, because spiders and beetles were showering into her face. Jessica wasn't screaming any more: her teeth were clenched with pain and effort as she tried to pull the robe's claws away from her arm.

It shook its hood and it howled at her, a howl that sounded as if it had come directly from every dark cellar that ever was. It bared its teeth and arched its hood back like a cobra, and she realized that it was about to tear her head off.

'Renko!' she panted. She didn't have the strength to scream. Renko gave the gate another desperate kick, and then another, and then he took three steps back, ready to rush at it. As he did so, however, a blood-red robe caught hold of his arm and tried to pull him away.

But Renko took judo classes. He rolled onto the ground, so that the robe toppled over his shoulder, and its full weight collided with the gate. With a loud clang the gate swung open.

Shadow Cats

Instantly, the night was flooded with brilliant sunshine. The red robe let out an appalling screech like a thousand chalkboards being scratched by ten thousand fingernails. It tried to climb upright, and for an instant Jessica could see its distorted, malevolent face, formed out of creases and folded lapels. Then it collapsed onto the ground and it was nothing but a robe – flat, empty, and harmless.

At the same time, the hooded robe that had been clawing at her collapsed too; and so did the jacket that had been trying to pull Elica into its bug-infested insides. All around them, in the sunshine, the robes dropped to the grass. There were dozens of them, and they looked as if luggage had fallen from a passing airplane and spilled all over the hill.

They turned toward the open gate. On the other side of it they could see a bone-white desert, with diamond-shaped bushes and diamond-shaped mountains in the far distance.

'Look – this was where Mrs Crawford went,' said Jessica, slowly walking toward it. 'The desert, the mountains. This is just the way she described it.'

'Are you all right?' asked Renko. 'Your arms are bleeding.'

Jessica looked down and saw that she had three or four long scratches on her upper arms, and several criss-cross scratches on her hands. Her wrists were bruised too, and she had broken three fingernails.

Elica had a red bruise on the side of her cheek and a pattern of bruises around her ankles, but otherwise she seemed to be unhurt. 'One day I fall into holly bush and this is not worse.'

Renko took hold of Jessica's hand. 'Are you sure you're going to be OK?'

'Yes . . . but I don't think we ought to go back the same way. Maybe we can try going through the desert.'

'So where does the desert lead?'

'To Mrs Crawford's old bedroom, I guess.'

'You guess? Supposing it doesn't?'

'If it doesn't, we'll have to go back the way we came, to my bedroom.'

'We'd better wait until it gets light. I don't fancy being torn to pieces by half of Ames's nightwear department.'

They stepped through the gate and into the desert. It was very hot here, and breathlessly silent. High above their heads, a flock of clothes hangers circled, as lazy as vultures.

'Which way do we go?' asked Renko.

'I don't know,' said Jessica. 'We should look for a door – a door just standing on its own.'

They shaded their eyes with their hands and scanned the horizon. The gate was still open, and they could still see the zigzag path and the heaps of robes lying on the hill. But there was no sign of a door anywhere.

'We should walk,' said Elica. 'Maybe we find somebody help us.'

'What, like a talking cactus?'

'It doesn't matter what, if it can show us a way.'

'Elica, it's real hot here, and there's nothing to drink. I don't feel like ending up as a heap of bones in a desert behind somebody's bedroom wallpaper.'

'What can we do? We have to try. My father always say, every journey take you somewhere.'

'What is he, your father, some kind of genius?'

They were still arguing about what to do when Jessica said, 'Ssh!' and then, 'Listen!' They stopped talking and listened, and very faintly they could hear the sound of a flute playing. It was the same melancholy music that Jessica had heard before, the sort of music that brings tears to your eyes although you don't know why.

'I think it's coming from over there,' said Renko, pointing to a collection of diamond-shaped rocks.

'Well, let's go take a look,' said Jessica. 'If there's music, somebody must be playing it.'

'Another genius. You guys are really beginning to make me feel very, very dim.'

They walked across the desert toward the rocks, their track-shoes crunching on the salty white surface. At first they couldn't see anybody, but as they skirted around the rocks they saw a frail white-haired woman in a rusty-colored robe, sitting cross-legged on the ground and playing a small bright silver flute. She stopped playing when she saw them, looked up, and smiled.

'So good to see you,' she said. 'I haven't seen anybody in years and years.'

She was quite a handsome woman, although her eyes were dull and her cheeks were sunken, like somebody who has been ill for a very long time.

'We're looking for the door,' said Jessica. 'We're wondering if you could show us the way.'

'Of course. It isn't difficult and it isn't far. Depending on your point of view, of course, and your personal circumstances.'

'Are you the lady that Mrs Crawford told me about?' Jessica asked her.

'Mrs Crawford? I don't know anybody by that name.'

'Oh, that's right. Her name wouldn't have been Crawford then. She was only a girl. Edwina.'

'Little Edwina! Yes, I remember little Edwina. She came to see me when she was very sick. I never found out what happened to her, because she never came back.'

'She got better. She's living in a house on the road to Allen's Corners. She says you gave her a ring.'

'I did, yes. My engagement ring. She was supposed to give it to my daughter Martha, as a sign that I was here, and that I was still alive.'

'I think she did. But I don't think your daughter believed her.'

'I see. Well, that's very sad. Sad for her and sad for me. Do you know if she's still alive?'

'I don't. My grandpa said that she disappeared, after all the children died.'

The old lady pressed her hand against her mouth. 'The children died? Oh no. Oh, that's terrible. I loved them so much. How did they die, do you know?'

'It was Rocky Mountain spotted fever. I'm sorry.'

'Oh, that distresses me so much.'

Renko said, 'I hate to interrupt, but what are those black things way over there?'

The old woman lifted her head to look; and then she stood up and looked again. 'We'll have to think about making a move. Those are shadow cats.'

'Shadow cats?'

'Cats made out of all the shadows you can see from the corner of your eye, and all the shadows on your bedroom ceiling. They're very quick – so quick that you can barely see them. But they're very vicious, too. They'll have your eyes out before you know it.'

'Maybe we'd better get trucking then,' said Renko.

The old woman put her flute in her pocket and lifted her hood to cover her head. 'This way,' she said. 'Walk as fast as you can and don't look back. There's nothing that riles a shadow cat more than being looked at.'

Together they began to walk as quickly as they could across the desert, toward a straggle of bushes with diamond-shaped leaves. Far to their left, Jessica could see the diamond-shaped mountains that Mrs Crawford had described. The heat haze on the horizon made them look as if they were floating on a bright silvery lake.

'So you're Mrs Pennington's mother?' she said, hobbling to keep up.

'That's right. Maude Fellowes. My husband Albert bought the house in 1919, and it was so big that when Martha married George Pennington in 1923 we invited them to live with us. All of Martha and George's children were born there, and they all loved it. It was a very happy house, believe me. You should have seen it at Christmas, with the tallest tree you can imagine, all shining with candles!'

Jessica was beginning to limp badly. She looked back over her shoulder to make sure that the shadow cats weren't catching up with them. 'Don't!' warned Mrs Fellowes. 'They're very touchy, those varmints! They only have to think that you're staring at them . . . !'

Renko came up to Jessica and took hold of her hand to help her along. 'How long have you been here?' he asked Mrs Fellowes. 'I mean, like, here in this desert?'

'An elephant's age and the blink of an eye, both. That's the way things are here. Sometimes it seems as if I came through the wallpaper just yesterday afternoon, and other times it feels as if I've been here since the beginning of time.'

'How did you get here?' asked Jessica.

'Yes,' said Elica. 'And why you not go back?'

'I was sick,' said Mrs Fellowes. 'More than just sick, I had a stomach tumor and I was dying. My poor husband was distraught, because there was nothing he could do to save me. I stayed in the small upstairs bedroom with my

116

nurse in the room next to me, so that at least poor Albert could get some rest.

'Then one night I woke up about two or three o'clock in the morning and the room was filled with light, and all the diamonds on the wallpaper were singing, like a heavenly choir. I swear I thought I was dead.

'I walked toward the wall and it was just as if welcoming hands were drawing me in. And that's when I found myself here.

'There was a young girl here when I first arrived. Her name was Renata, and she was the daughter of the previous owners. Pretty girl she was, very pale skin and coppery hair. She said that she had caught consumption, and she was dying like I was, but the wallpaper had taken her in. She hadn't got better, but she hadn't gotten any worse, and she was waiting for the time when consumption could be cured, so that she could go back. She asked me if anyone had found a way to cure it yet, and I had to say no, they hadn't.'

'They have now,' said Jessica. 'I had a vaccination against it when I was eleven.'

'If only I knew where Renata went . . . I haven't seen her in years. Or is it weeks? Or is it just a few days? I find it very hard to remember.'

A door had appeared up ahead of them, a simple bedroom door of plain scrubbed deal with a shiny brass handle. Just as Mrs Crawford had described it, it stood in the middle of the desert with nothing around it, a bedroom door without a bedroom.

'Of course I have to ask you,' said Mrs Fellowes: 'if they've found a cure for consumption, dare I know if they've found a cure for cancer?'

'There are plenty of treatments for cancer,' said Jessica.

'My doctor said that mine was too far gone to be treatable.'

'But when was that? Way back before World War Two. They have all kinds of new treatments now.'

'I couldn't stand any more treatments. Here, at least I don't feel any pain.'

'Why don't you come back with us and we'll take you to the doctor, so that you can have a check-up?'

Mrs Fellowes shook her head. 'Why don't you come back and find me when they discover a cure?'

They were only fifty feet away from the door now, and their pace was starting to slow. Jessica said, 'How can I leave you here, all alone? They may never find a cure.'

Mrs Fellowes reached out and held both of Jessica's hands. Her eyes were dull but she managed a smile. 'There are many dangers here, but there is happiness and peace of a kind which you can only imagine.'

'Aren't you lonely?'

'Yes, I am. But I have my flute, and the days roll by like a wheel.'

'Come back with us,' Jessica pleaded. 'I'm sure that Dr Leeming could make you better.'

Again Mrs Fellowes shook her head. 'Albert is dead, my grandchildren are all dead. I suppose Martha is dead too.'

'She disappeared, that's what my grandpa said.'

'Poor Martha. She adored those children. She worshipped every hair on their heads.'

They had almost reached the door. But as they did so Jessica glimpsed something out of the corner of her eye, something black and very quick. The next thing she knew, three shadowy creatures had sprung between them and the door, and were crouched there, their claws spread, their teeth bared, their eyes as yellow as pus.

'Shadow cats,' said Mrs Fellowes. 'Stay still, try not to look at them directly.'

Jessica found it almost impossible to look at them directly, even if she tried. They were big, almost as big as pumas, but their outline was smudged and somehow she couldn't focus on them. When she turned her head, she caught sight of one of them out of the very corner of her eye, but then it was gone. Mrs Fellowes was right: they were the restless shadows on the bedroom ceiling on a stormy night. They were the shadows of rooks flying across a wintry lawn. They were black as smoke and sinister as cellars.

'Stay as still as statues,' Mrs Fellowes cautioned them. 'I'm going to draw them away from the door . . . when I do, I want all three of you to open it up and run inside and close it behind you, quick.'

'But what's going to happen to you?'

'You never mind me. I've met shadow cats plenty of times before.'

'But you said they'd tear your eyes out.'

'Just you do as I tell you. You want to get back, don't you? This is the only way.'

Without warning, one of the shadow cats ran around behind Jessica and clawed at her back. 'Aah!' she cried out. She felt as if she had been lashed with barbed wire. She turned around, but the shadow cat had flickered away. It suddenly jumped up at Elica, snagging her plaits and scratching her ear.

'Here, you cowardly creatures!' Mrs Fellowes shouted out, waving her arms. 'Here, you black-hearted beasts!'

'No!' said Jessica. 'You can't!'

'I can and I am,' Mrs Fellowes retorted, fixing Jessica with a defiant stare. 'Who cares what happens to me? What have I got to look forward to? More treatment? More pain? More long years in the desert?'

A shadow cat came running up to her long and low, its belly close to the ground. It was just like the shadow of a real cat, running beside a garden wall, distorted by every bump and ripple in the brick.

'Look out!' shouted Renko hoarsely; and it was then that Mrs Fellowes turned to face it directly.

Out in the Snow

Mrs Fellowes' stare stopped the shadow cat in its tracks. It lowered its head even further, arched its back and raised a tail that looked like a twist of black smoke. Mrs Fellowes held her ground, never taking her eyes off it.

'Go on,' she told Jessica. 'Now's your chance. Through the door, quick as you can, and close it behind you.'

Renko said, 'There's no way.'

But Mrs Fellowes shrilled out, 'Now! Do it now! Before it's too late!'

At that instant the shadow cat pounced on her. It ripped her hood off and attacked her face. Jessica saw its claws pierce her eye-sockets and drag both of her eyes out onto her cheeks, two bloody ping-pong balls. Another shadow cat leaped onto her back, and three more went for her legs and arms. She fell to the ground, not screaming, not even crying out, while the dark flickering shapes clawed and bit at her flesh. Blood flew everywhere, as if it were being sprayed by a garden sprinkler.

Jessica stood watching this horror with her mouth open, but suddenly she felt Renko seizing her hand and pulling her toward the door. Elica had opened it, and beyond the door was an empty, brightly lit room. The last that Jessica saw of Mrs Fellowes was one bloody arm waving at her like a rag doll.

They pushed their way into the room and Renko slammed

the door behind them. They stared at each other, panting.
There were squiggles of blood on Jessica's face and hands.

'She did that for us,' said Elica, and she was shivering
and crying. 'She let them kill her, for saving us!'

Renko put his arm around her and said, 'There's nothing
we can do now. Let's get back, before we get chased by
something else.'

They went to the opposite wall and stood facing it. Dimly,
through the diamond-patterned wallpaper, they could see the
bedroom beyond, with an iron bed and a nightstand and a
chest of drawers with a jug and basin on top of it.

'Ready?' said Jessica. Behind them they heard something
heavy thump against the door, and the furious scrabbling of
claws. Another thump, and a vicious snarl.

Together, tightly holding hands, they stepped through
the wallpaper. This bedroom was damp and cold, because
Jessica's grandparents didn't use it any more, and it was
illuminated only by the moon gleaming on the snow outside. They took one look back at the diamond-patterned
wallpaper and Jessica said, 'I never saw anything so terrible, ever.'

'She let them tear her to pieces,' said Renko. 'I can't
believe she did that.'

'She will go in heaven now,' added Elica.

And Jessica said, 'Amen.'

Jessica switched on her computer. She logged on to the
Internet, and typed in 'spotted fever'. Immediately she was
presented with page after page of medical details.

'Look at all this,' said Renko. 'I can't believe I never
heard of spotted fever before.'

'See,' said Jessica, pointing at the screen. 'It's usually
called Rocky Mountain spotted fever – RMSF for short.
It says here that it's one of the fastest-growing infectious
diseases amongst young people in America. Look – over

two-thirds of the people who contract RMSF are under the age of fifteen.'

'How do you catch it?' asked Renko.

'Hold on – here it is. In western states it's carried by the wood tick, and the dog tick carries it in the east. You get bitten by the tick, and the bacillus gets into your bloodstream. You get a rash, and a headache, then you get mental confusion and finally you die of heart failure.'

'Can it be cured?'

'These days, yes, if you catch it in the first few days. It says here that one dose of doxycycline can practically cure you overnight.'

'So we could probably save those children before the Stain gets them.'

'I think so,' said Jessica. 'At least we ought to try.'

They tried to sleep but it wasn't easy, with bloody images of Mrs Fellowes in their mind's eye. Twice Jessica woke up to find herself hitting her pillow as if she were fighting off a shadow cat. At eight o'clock Grannie came around to their bedrooms and woke them for breakfast. Outside it was snowing again, thicker than ever, and the world was breathlessly silent. Over pancakes with syrup and crispy bacon, they discussed what they could do next.

'We have to find out if Dr Leeming has any doxycycline,' said Jessica. 'If he does, we can get the children out through the wallpaper and take them to see him.'

'But won't he want to know who they are, and where their parents are?'

'Of course he will. But we can say they're cousins of mine, come for a visit. He won't refuse to cure them, will he? We can worry about explanations when they're better.'

'Nobody will be believing us,' said Elica solemnly.

'I don't think that matters, does it? What matters is saving their lives.'

'In that case, let's call up Dr Leeming and ask him.'

Jessica picked up the phone, but the heavy snow must have brought the lines down, because all she heard was a continuous sizzling noise. Renko said, 'It's OK, I'll use my cellphone.' But he couldn't get a signal either.

'We will have to walk on our legs,' said Elica.

Jessica put on the long brown old-fashioned coat with the black-velvet collar that she had bought at a thrift store in Washington Depot. They were wrapping themselves in their scarves and tugging on their gloves when Grace arrived, with Epiphany. 'It's snowing so bad out there,' said Grace. 'I heard that all the roads to Washington Depot are closed, and they got the snow-plows coming over from Waterbury. You taking a walk? In this? You got to be real gluttons for punishment.'

'We're only going to New Milford,' said Jessica.

'I'll come,' enthused Epiphany.

'You have your math homework to finish,' Grace told her.

'Oh please, Mom, I can do my homework later.'

'When you're watching TV?'

'I'll do it, Mom, I promise you.'

'OK then. But make sure you're back in time for lunch.'

The four of them stepped out into a soundless world of whirling white. Jessica introduced Epiphany to Renko and Elica and then swore her to secrecy.

'So what's so secret?'

'We went through the wallpaper.'

'Come on, you're kidding me.'

'We went through the wallpaper, it's true. There's a whole different world in there. I promise you, we're not making it up.'

'You're not kidding me? You really went? There's a world there, really? You got to be kidding me.'

'God's-honest truth,' Renko assured her. 'I wouldn't have believed it myself if I hadn't done it.'

'Well, I saw what Mrs Crawford did with that waterlily on her carpet . . .'

Jessica told her all about Phoebe and the Stain. 'It's all real, Piff, I swear it. That's why we're going to New Milford, to make sure that Dr Leeming can cure Phoebe and her brothers and sisters if we bring them out of there.'

'And this Stain? What exactly is that?'

'We're not sure. But everybody seems to think it's the worst possible thing in the world.'

'You mean there's something worse than men?'

'Hey,' said Renko.

'You're excused,' Epiphany told him. 'You're not your typical macho stuff-strutting bigot.'

'Well thanks.'

They passed Mrs Crawford's house, almost buried under a deep mantle of snow, with only a single light in the living-room window to show that there was anybody home. Then they crossed the road to Allen's Corners Cemetery. 'We might as well go through here,' Jessica suggested. 'It's much quicker, and my toes are getting seriously cold.'

They opened the cast-iron gates and walked along an avenue of black granite tombstones and pale limestone angels with lifted wings. 'I think I'd rather be cremated when I die,' said Epiphany. 'At least it'll be warm.'

They had almost reached the other side of the cemetery when Jessica stopped and pointed. 'Look at that. One of the roses said that I'd find the children's names where the gray woman in the green cloak stands and weeps.'

Close to the wall stood an angel with her head bowed and her wings folded. She must have been facing north, because over the years a thick cloak of moss had gathered on her back.

Jessica went over to the angel and brushed the flecks of

snow off her plinth. The inscription on it read IN MEMORY OF THE PENNINGTON CHILDREN, TAKEN AWAY FROM US JULY 24TH 1937, MARTIN, MARGARET, DAVID, JOEL AND PHOEBE. MAY THE ANGELS TAKE GOOD CARE OF THEM.

'So the children in the wall are the Pennington children,' said Epiphany. 'When they got sick their parents must have taken them into the wallpaper to save their lives . . . keeping them there till somebody found a cure.'

'But how would they have known how to do that?' asked Renko.

'Don't you remember?' cried Jessica. 'When she was sick, Mrs Crawford met the children's grandmother, Mrs Fellowes, behind the wallpaper. Mrs Fellowes gave Mrs Crawford her sapphire ring, so that she could take it to Mrs Pennington to prove that she was really there. Maybe Mrs Pennington didn't believe her. You remember that Mrs Crawford said that she was really, really angry. But when her five children all got sick with the spotted fever, she probably decided that it was worth trying anything to keep them alive.'

'And you hear what Phoebe say,' put in Elica. 'Her parents come again and again through the wallpaper with medicine, but none of medicine is working. Then they don't come anymore.'

'Poor Mrs Fellowes,' said Jessica. 'She died without knowing that her grandchildren are all still alive . . . and so close to her, through the gate by the stained-glass cottage.'

'This gets weirder and weirder,' said Epiphany.

'I know, but if you come with us next time we go through the wallpaper, you'll see that it makes some kind of peculiar sense. There's a pattern to it. It's, like, wallpaper patterns keep on repeating themselves, over and over, and I guess that's what happens in the world behind the wallpaper. Every day repeats itself, so that if you're sick you don't get better but you never get sicker. You never get older, either. You're just the same, forever and ever.'

They crossed the blinding-white snow-covered green in the middle of New Milford and went through the open gate into Dr Leeming's single-story clinic. There was only one person waiting to see the doctor, old Mr Steinberg from the hardware store, with his usual disgusting cough, so it wasn't long before Dr Leeming called them in to see him.

'Well, Jessica, and what brings you out on a horrible cold day like today?'

'I just wanted to make sure that you had some doxycycline.'

'Doxycycline? Yes, as a matter of fact I do.'

'Enough for five people?'

Dr Leeming cocked his head on one side, smiling at Jessica quizzically. 'Five people suffering from what, exactly?'

'Nothing in particular. I just wanted to know if you had any.'

'Doxycycline is one of the tetracyclines. We use it to kill off a whole range of bacteria, as well as some of the rickettsia, which are halfway between bacteria and viruses. We use it against viruses, too, like psittacosis, which you can catch from parrots. You don't know five people who have been pecked by parrots, do you?'

'Oh, no, nothing like that.'

Dr Leeming waited for her to say something else, but now that he had told her everything she needed to know all she could do was give him an inane smile.

'You're not sick in any way yourself?'

'Oh, no, I'm fine.'

His receptionist knocked and came in, and he looked beyond her through the open door to the waiting-room. 'And none of your friends is sick?'

'No, they're great.'

'All right, then,' said Dr Leeming. 'Unless there's anything else, I have some house-calls to make.'

'Oh . . . what time will you be back?'

'Around five, I guess, depending on the weather. Why?'

'No reason, really. Maybe I'll see you later.'

'I hope not. Especially not if you're suffering from anything that needs treatment with doxycycline!'

The four of them left the surgery and headed back toward home. It was snowing even more furiously now, as if even the weather could sense that something frightening was about to happen.

Angel of Mercy

They walked back through the cemetery. Alone in the snow, the angel that watched over the Pennington children's monument looked even sadder and more abandoned than ever.

'I'm freezing,' complained Epiphany. 'I'm going to run.'

'You go ahead then,' said Jessica. 'Ask my granny if she could have a hot drink ready for us. She makes lovely hot chocolate with cocoa powder on it.'

Epiphany went jogging on in front of them, kicking up snow as she ran. Jessica, Renko and Elica stayed together. They were all too tired to run, and still upset by what had happened to Mrs Fellowes, and Jessica's ankle was very sore.

'What if we can't get the children out of the wallpaper until after the doctor's surgery closes?' asked Renko.

'I know where Dr Leeming lives. We can take them there.'

'They will be need shoes, and coats,' Elica pointed out.

'I think I've got enough,' said Jessica. 'And if the older boys are too big, they can borrow Grandpa Willy's shoes.'

Epiphany had reached the cemetery gates. She turned and waved, then went running off across the road.

Jessica saw it as if it were a dream. A large black car appeared through the whirling snow, its headlights gleaming. The driver was going far too fast, and he didn't see Epiphany until it was too late. Even from this distance,

129

Jessica heard a dull thump, and Epiphany flew up into the air as if performing an amazing high-jump. Then she dropped to the ground and rolled over as the car went speeding off into the storm without stopping.

'Piff!' screamed Jessica. Renko and Elica went running off toward the gates, while Jessica limped after them as fast as she could.

When they reached her, Epiphany was lying on her back in the snow, her arms spread wide, her left leg awkwardly folded under her right. There was a wide graze on her forehead and her eyes were closed.

Jessica knelt down beside her and took hold of her hand. 'Piff! Can you hear me? Piff, are you all right? Please open your eyes, please!'

Renko leaned right over her. 'She's still breathing, but she sounds like she's having trouble.'

At that moment, a thin runnel of red blood welled up in the side of Epiphany's mouth and slid down onto the snow.

'I think her ribs could be broken,' said Renko. 'Maybe she's punctured a lung.'

He unbuttoned his coat, took out his cellphone and dialed 911. He listened, shook the phone, and then he said, 'Nothing. No signal at all.'

'Try it again,' Jessica urged him. 'If she's punctured a lung, she could suffocate.'

Renko tried switching his phone off and then back on again, but there was still no signal.

'What do we do?' asked Elica, desperately. 'There is no cars, nobody coming.'

'Run to Mrs Crawford's house,' said Jessica. 'Knock on her door and tell her what's happened. Maybe her phone's working.'

Elica got up and ran as fast as she could through Mrs Crawford's snowbound garden. Jessica could hear her banging frantically at the doorknocker. Meanwhile Epiphany coughed and more blood poured out of the side of her mouth.

'Hold on, Piff. Elica's gone for help. Please hold on.'

She saw Mrs Crawford opening her front door and Elica explaining what had happened. Mrs Crawford went back inside for a while and then she reappeared wearing a black overcoat and a ratty fur hat and carrying a fawn trenchcoat over her arm. She and Elica came hurrying over.

'Oh dear God,' she said when she saw Epiphany. 'And the car didn't even stop? Some people are totally inhuman.'

'What are we going to do?' asked Jessica. 'Renko's phone won't work and there's nobody around anywhere at all.'

'My phone won't work either,' said Mrs Crawford. 'You're not supposed to move people after accidents, especially when they're bleeding, but I don't think we have any choice, do you? We can carry her in this raincoat, that should make a sort of a stretcher. Renko – is that your name? – do you know where Dr Leeming's surgery is? Run and get him as fast as you can.'

'We've just come from there,' Jessica told her. 'He's out making house-calls.'

Epiphany coughed again, and groaned, but she still didn't open her eyes. Mrs Crawford took hold of her wrist and felt her pulse. 'Very thready. She needs help now.'

'She will not die?' asked Elica.

'I think she's been hurt quite badly.'

'We can't let her die,' said Jessica. 'We can't!'

Mrs Crawford put her hand over her mouth and thought for a moment, and then she said, 'There's only one thing we can do. We'll take her back to your house, and we'll take her through the wallpaper.'

'What?' said Renko.

'It won't cure her, but she won't get any worse, and she can stay there until we can call for an ambulance.'

'This is nuts.'

'Yes, maybe it is, but do you have a better idea?'

Renko frowned. 'Well . . . no, I guess I don't.'

'Let's get on with it, then. Jessica, if I lift her up a little, can you slide the raincoat underneath her . . . and then Renko and Elica, can you pull it through from the other side?'

Mrs Crawford took Epiphany in both arms and raised her as gently as if she were her own baby. Jessica pushed the raincoat underneath her back, and when Mrs Crawford tilted Epiphany the other way Renko and Elica were able to drag it through. Now Mrs Crawford and Renko took an epaulet each, while Jessica and Elica held onto the coat-tails, and between them they were able to lift Epiphany off the snow and carry her, like an African explorer being toted through the bush by native bearers.

Epiphany was only a skinny girl, but as they trudged along the road toward Jessica's house she felt heavier and heavier, and Jessica had to twist the raincoat and grip it with both hands to stop herself from dropping it.

'What are you going to tell Piff's mother?' Renko panted. 'She's not going to let you take Piff into the wallpaper, is she? And I don't suppose your grandparents are going to be too understanding about it either.'

'I've thought about that,' said Jessica. 'We'll go in the back door and up the servants' stairs. Grace should still be in the kitchen, and Grannie and Grandpa Willy usually have a cup of coffee in the living-room about now.'

'I'm going to have to lay her down for a moment,' said Mrs Crawford. 'I'm not a spring chicken anymore.'

They had reached the gate that would take them through the garden and up to the back door. Mrs Crawford leaned against the gatepost, her face white but her cheeks flushed with pink, and a drip on the end of her nose. She wiped the drip with her woolly glove and then she said, 'All right. I think I can make one more effort.'

Between them they lifted Epiphany up again and carried her across the garden. The snow came up to their knees, so they had to high-step like circus ponies. In the middle of the garden the statue of Pan watched them and grinned. The god of unreasonable fear, the god of panic. Jessica thought: We can't panic, we have to be calm. We can't let Epiphany die.

They opened the back door and carried Epiphany into the black-and-white-tiled scullery, where Grannie kept her old-fashioned twin-tub washing-machine, and sheets and pillowcases hung damply from the ceiling to dry. After she had closed the door behind them, Jessica listened, but all she could hear was Grace singing in the kitchen.

'Come on,' she urged. 'As quick as we can.'

Climbing the staircase was almost more than they could manage, and twice Mrs Crawford lost her footing and nearly fell. What was more, the staircase groaned loudly with every step they took, and the door to the living-room was half open, so Jessica expected her granny to appear any moment and ask them what on earth they were doing.

Epiphany murmured something as they turned the bend in the stairs, and half lifted her hand, but there was nothing Jessica could do to comfort her: it was all that she could do to hold onto the raincoat.

At last they managed to reach the landing and shuffle across to Jessica's bedroom. Renko pushed the door open with his shoulder, and they carried Epiphany inside and laid her on the bed.

'She looks bad,' said Mrs Crawford. Epiphany's face was an ashy gray and she was breathing with a choky catch in her throat. 'Try your cellphone again, Renko – and Jessica, try the ordinary phone.'

Renko prodded at his cellphone again, listened and shook

his head. Jessica tiptoed to her grandparents' bedroom and picked up the old white telephone on the nightstand, but there was still nothing but an endless sizzle, like somebody frying bacon.

She came back to her bedroom and said, 'The lines are still down. I won't be able to send an e-mail, either. We'll have to take her through.'

'What about the Stain?' asked Renko. 'It's supposed to leak out at eleven o'clock tonight.'

'That's not for hours. The phones will be working before then. Just as long as we can keep Piff comfortable until we can call the paramedics.'

'The Stain?' said Mrs Crawford. 'What's that?'

'There were these beings behind the wallpaper,' Jessica explained. 'They were like very bright lights. They called themselves the Light People. They said that there's something terrible called the Stain which is going to leak out tonight and take over the whole world inside the wall. They said it's the worst thing in the world, the worst thing you could ever imagine.'

'Well, I did warn you, didn't I, that there are all kinds of dangers inside the wall?'

Elica began to say, 'Yes, we saw cats – cats like shadows—' But Jessica gave her a quick warning look and shook her head. This wasn't the time to be telling Mrs Crawford about what had happened to Mrs Fellowes.

Mrs Crawford said, 'Now then, let's get this poor girl into the pattern, without any more delay.'

Between them, they lifted up the raincoat again, and carried Epiphany toward the flowery wallpaper. Jessica and Renko pushed through first, and Elica and Mrs Crawford followed. There was a moment when Epiphany was half in and half out of the wall, and Jessica could only dimly see Elica and Mrs Crawford in the bedroom they had left behind. Then they were all standing in the overgrown garden, in brilliant sunshine, under high white clouds that were formed from crumpled pillowcases.

They laid Epiphany down on the lawn, amongst the daisies. She seemed to be sleeping now, and the bleeding from her mouth appeared to have stopped, although Jessica was still worried that she might have been injured internally. At least she wouldn't get any worse, not while she was here inside the wallpaper.

'Maybe we should put her in the shade,' Renko suggested. 'Under that tree would be a good place.'

But they were just about to pick her up when five or six tall blue irises came walking toward them through the long grass, swaying gently as they approached, like very thin nuns. Like the roses', their petals formed faces, although these weren't crumpled and cantankerous like the roses were. They were serene, detached, as you would expect the faces of nuns to be, the Sisters of the Holy Flag.

'Your friend is hurt,' said one of the irises, in a watery, clearly enunciated voice.

Mrs Crawford looked startled, but Jessica said, 'It's all right. All the flowers talk here.' Then she turned back to the iris. 'We've brought her here because it's snowing back in our world, and we can't get help.'

'Then you must take her to the proper place,' replied the iris. 'A place where she will be watched over, and cared for.'

'Where's that?'

'Follow us, and we will show you.'

The irises began to walk off in slow procession, singing as they went, a song that sounded almost like a hymn. Jessica said, 'I suppose we'd better follow them,' and so they picked up Epiphany yet again and carried her through the garden, between rows of dark green bushes that smelled strongly of eucalyptus. Each bush was dotted with different flowers from Grannie's summer dresses, pink, white, yellow and scarlet.

It wasn't long before they arrived in a neatly trimmed garden surrounded by hedges. Actually it looked more like a private cemetery than a garden, because there were granite markers and stone crosses, and benches where people could sit and contemplate. In the very center of the garden stood the angel that had presided over the memorial to the Pennington children – or another angel that was very much like her. The irises led them toward her, and then said, 'You can lay your friend down here.'

Jessica shaded her eyes against the sunshine and looked up at the angel standing on her plinth. She had such a sad, beautiful face, and long robes, and feathered wings that almost touched the ground. Jessica was about to turn away when the angel opened her eyelids and smiled at her. It gave Jessica such a shock that she felt as if centipedes were scuttling down the back of her neck.

'Don't be afraid,' said the angel. Even though her eyes were open, her eyeballs were as gray as the stone from which she was carved, so that she looked as if she were blind.

'I'm – I'm not afraid,' said Jessica.

'I will take care of your friend, I promise you, until you can find help.'

Elica crossed herself, and even Renko was shaken.

'I must warn you, though, that the Stain will soon appear and darken this world forever, and so you must be quick.'

'Don't you know how to stop it?'

'There is no way to stop the greatest evil that man can ever commit.'

'I have to find the Pennington children, too. I've found out how to cure them. I can take them out of here before it's too late.'

'There may not be time,' said the angel.

'But I can't leave them here, can I, if the Stain's going to take them?'

'You have no choice, my darling, if you wish to leave this world alive.'

Over the Lake

Jessica looked up. Already she could see that the sun had passed its zenith, and that the pillowcase-clouds were beginning to thicken. A chilly breeze blew through the garden, and there was a feeling that night was approaching much faster than it should have done.

'I promised,' she said. 'They're waiting for me to come back and save them.'

'Then you will have to travel as far and as fast as you can,' said the angel. 'The Stain is already starting to leak out from the east, and you won't be able to go by the most direct route. If it cuts you off, you will never be able to get back here before the Final Darkness and you, too, will be swallowed up.'

'I can try,' said Jessica. 'I have to try.'

'We come with you,' Elica asserted. 'We say, ha, Stain! Who cares about you? We spit on you!'

'You might as well spit into the widest and blackest of oceans,' said the angel. She had such a tired, regretful voice, she sounded as if she were going to cry. 'The Stain is what happens when evil goes unrepented and unpunished.'

'What evil?' asked Mrs Crawford. 'What could possibly have happened here in this house to create something like the Stain?'

'Only the flowers on the wallpaper know what happened,' said the angel. 'Only the bronze eyes of the great god Pan and the stone eyes of seraphim.'

'So *you* know? What did happen?'

'After the Pennington children were carried here, their father and mother did everything they possibly could to make them well again. However, they could never find a medicine that cured them. When year after year went by, and there was still no cure, Martha Pennington began to think that it would be better to give them something to help them to die. She couldn't bear to think of them being ill forever and ever, and she was terrified about what would happen when she and her husband grew old and passed away. Their children would be castaways, never ageing but eternally ill, in a world inside a wallpaper pattern.

'Her husband disagreed with her furiously. He said that they should never give up hope. But one night, while he was asleep, Martha Pennington passed through the wallpaper and gave each of her children an overdose of a very strong sedative, telling them that it was a miracle cure.

'They had already fallen into a deep coma when her husband woke up and discovered where she had gone and what she had done. He believed that she had killed all five of their children, and he pursued her, past the river, up the hill and back through the overgrown garden. She just managed to get back through the wallpaper, but her husband caught up with her.

'Who witnessed what happened next? Only the shining brass face of the clock on the mantelpiece. Only the roses, irises and blessed thistles. Only the wooden wolves in the closet doors and the shadow cats in the darkest of corners. Only the robes.

'George Pennington caught his wife and stabbed her so many times that she was smothered in red from head to foot. Smothered, as if she had been rolling in red paint.

'To hide her body, he carried her back through the wallpaper and buried her here. There – beyond the hedges and up the hill, where that black tree stands.'

The black tree was actually made of the wrought-iron curlicues from the gate in Grandpa Willy's garden. It looked bleak and weird, and the sky behind it was the color of bruised plums.

'What happened to the children?' asked Mrs Crawford.

'They were in such a deep sleep that George Pennington was convinced they were dead. He made wax impressions out of each of their faces so that he would always be able to remember what they looked like. They didn't stir, even then. After that he went back through the wallpaper and never came back.'

'Does anybody know what he did then?'

'He took to drinking. In the end he sold the house to your great-grandfather and then – who knows where he went? I am not a recording angel, but I would say that he probably died years ago.'

'So the Stain—'

'The Stain is the evil deed that George Pennington committed, and for which he was never sorry. It has grown into a thing that has a terrible life of its own, and it has grown blacker and blacker over the years, very slowly but very surely, and now it is rising up from under the ground and it will overwhelm everything. All of this pattern, all of this world, all of these hills and seas and gardens. There will be nothing here but darkness and emptiness.'

'What's the quickest way for us to get to the Pennington children?' asked Renko.

The angel lifted one stone wing, and pointed to the west. 'Go as far as the painted lake, then go north through the forest. On the other side of the forest is a house of mirrors where the children live.'

'A house of mirrors? You mean, like a funhouse?'

The angel shook her head. 'You will see when you find it. Bless you, and have a safe journey, and go as fast as your feet can take you.'

Mrs Crawford said, 'I'm afraid I'm too old for this kind of thing, Jessica. But I'll stay here and take care of Piff, and I'll go back through the wallpaper every now and then to see if the phone lines are back up.'

Jessica took hold of her hand and gave her a kiss on the cheek. 'Thank you. You don't know what a help you've been. We could never have done this without you.'

'Go quickly,' Mrs Crawford urged her. 'You don't want that evil Stain catching up with you.'

They left the cemetery-garden and started to walk up a steep, craggy hill. The crags were pieces of crazy paving from Grandpa Willy's garden, and the thick olive-green grass from which they protruded were the fringes from Grannie's green velvet couch.

The wind whipped their hair. Up above them the sky was slowly changing to a thin, diluted blue, and in the far distance a flock of teaspoons glittered in the fading sunlight. Ahead of them Jessica could see a low range of hills, and off to their right, toward the east, she could still see the curly black tree where the Stain was going to leak out. Behind the tree, the clouds were even darker, and she was sure that she could make out a blackness on top of the hill, as if waste oil were welling through the heather.

There was something else too. Occasionally she caught a scorched, sweetish smell on the wind, like burning garbage, only worse.

'Do you smell that?' she asked Renko as she hobbled over the rocks.

Renko sniffed and said, 'Yeah. Reminds me of the last time my old man tried to barbecue pork chops. My mom said he should apply for a job at the crematorium.'

'Are you all right, Jessica?' Elica asked her. 'Your foot does not hurt?'

'Some, but I'll make it. I should have brought my stick.'

They passed a bush that was made out of decorative

mahogany banister rails. Renko managed to crack one of the railings off, and gave it to her. 'There. One stick.'

The railing was a little too long and a little too heavy, but at least it allowed her to take some of the weight off her ankle. She hopped over the crags like Long John Silver.

'All you need now is an eye-patch and a parrot on your shoulder,' grinned Renko.

When they reached the crest of the crags they saw a lake below them, shining in the afternoon sun. Jessica recognized it immediately: it was Lake Waramaug, from an oil painting which hung over the fireplace. Grannie and Grandpa Willy had bought it along with the house. They descended the long slope toward the shoreline, and Jessica could see the cluster of small fishing-boats beside the pier and the wagon standing axle-deep in the water on the lake's far side.

The strange thing was, though, that it didn't feel chilly, like a real lake; and it didn't even smell like a real lake. There were seven or eight bafflehead ducks in the water, but they weren't moving. Elica ran toward them, clapping her hands, but they remained exactly where they were, not swimming, not quacking, not trying to fly away.

Jessica limped nearer to the shoreline. She peered closely at the ducks, and then she knelt down and touched the water itself. 'It's not wet,' she said. 'It's painted. This is nothing but a painting.'

Renko touched it too. Then he leaned over and stroked one of the ducks. 'How about that? Even the ducks are painted. But they sure look real, don't they?'

'We'd better keep going,' said Jessica. 'Where did the angel say we had to go next?'

'Through the forest. That must be it, on the other side of the lake.'

'It's going to take us an hour to walk around.'

'Why should it? This isn't water, it's oil paint, and what's more, it's dry oil paint.'

'Sure.' Renko held out both hands, one to Jessica and the other to Elica. 'If we can see teaspoons flying south for the winter, I don't exactly think that the usual laws of physics apply here, do you?'

He took one step out onto the water. It made a faint crackling sound, but that was all. 'See? It supports my weight. Come on, what are you afraid of?'

Elica put out one pointed toe like a ballet dancer. Then she too stepped onto the water. She took another step, and then another, and did a little pirouette. 'It is fine! It is quite fine! Jessica, you must come, also!'

Jessica prodded the water with her banister rail. It felt perfectly solid, except for the slightest 'give', like canvas. She swung her good foot out, and then her lame foot, and soon she was following Renko and Elica past the motionless, shiny-feathered ducks, past the fishing-boats, past the pier and the mooring-posts and the jagged black rocks along the shoreline, out across the surface of the lake itself. Jessica looked down and saw that the water had been painted in so many different blues and greens, and even purples, and every now and then they would have to step over a thick crusting of white paint which represented foam.

'I just wonder,' she said, as they came near to reaching the center of the lake, 'do you think that if Grannie and Grandpa Willy went into the dining-room now, and looked at this painting, they could see us walking across it?'

'Don't start getting all deep on me now,' said Renko. He checked his wristwatch. 'It's way past five o'clock already and we haven't even found the house yet.'

It took them another ten minutes to walk to the farther shore. The forest came almost down to the water's edge, and the trees were very tall, so tall that Jessica had to crane her neck back to see the tops of them. They were dark, too, with trunks that looked as if they were deeply folded and bark that was mottled with maroons and browns and rich purples. It was only when they came nearer that Jessica could see that they were not really trees at all but velvet curtains, and that the rumpled foliage high above their heads which blotted out the afternoon sunshine was pelmets and swags.

As they entered the gloom of the forest, the trees actually swayed like curtains, and they had only gone a short distance before they found that they were enveloped in almost total darkness. The air was stuffy, like Grannie's living-room, and Jessica began to feel a rising sense of claustrophobia.

'How do we get through here?' asked Elica, pushing against the nearest tree. 'It is so dark and we do not know which way.'

'I forgot to bring my flashlight,' said Jessica. 'Maybe we'd better go back to the lake and try to find a way around the forest, instead of through it.'

'But you saw the size of it,' put in Renko. 'It could take us hours and hours.'

They were still deciding what to do when Jessica glimpsed a thin bright light shining between the trees. It vanished, and there was darkness again, but then it reappeared, a dazzling vertical ray, like the sun coming through her bedroom curtains in the morning.

'Wait,' she told Renko and Elica. 'It's the Light People. Look – they've come to help us.'

The light grew brighter and brighter until they had to shield their eyes with their hands. One of the Light People appeared between the trees, a brilliant filament with wings of wriggling incandescence.

'Where are you going?' it asked them, hovering and dancing around them. 'The Stain is leaking out already, you have to go back.'

'We're going to save the Pennington children. We're on our way there now.'

'There won't be time,' said the light-fairy, in its plink-plankety music-box voice. 'The Stain will be here in less

144

than an hour; and less than an hour after that, the whole of this pattern will be nothing but darkness and miasma.'

'You have asthma?' asked Renko, bewildered.

'No . . . "miasma" means a poisonous atmosphere that rises from anything rotting and causes evil and disease. There won't be anything left here but a swampy wasteland, completely without beauty, completely without light.'

'But what about the Pennington children . . . their parents left them here so that they would stay alive, and if I can get them out of here, I know a way to make them better!'

The light-fairy dimmed dull orange for a moment, like a flashlight that is starting to lose its charge. 'There is nothing you can do. There isn't time. Besides, this forest is very dangerous.'

'*Cu le frica de orice nor nici o calatone nu face,*' said Elica. 'If you are afraid of leaves you shouldn't go into the woods.'

'You don't have to be concerned about leaves in this forest,' retorted the light-fairy. 'But you do have to watch for wooden wolves and shadow cats and all kinds of other ugly patterns and shapes.'

'Doesn't matter,' said Renko. 'We promised the Pennington kids that we were going to save them and that's exactly what we're going to do.'

The light-fairy didn't answer at first, but dipped and flickered like a giant firefly. At last it said, 'You'd better follow me then. As quickly as you possibly can.'

Immediately it floated off between the tall, swaying trees, so that shafts of brilliant light fanned out in all directions. Renko put his hand on Jessica's shoulder and said, 'We could always go back, you know.'

'After what you just said?'

'Supposing that light dude is right, and there really isn't enough time?'

Jessica said, 'When my parents were killed, I nearly

145

died too, but the doctors managed to save me. Then I fell downstairs and hit my head because you and Sue-Anne were bullying me, and that was when I first heard the children's voices. I think I was saved for a reason, and I think I hit my head for a reason, and that was to save Phoebe and all her brothers and sisters. Even if you don't want to go any further, Renko, I have to. I won't think you're chicken or anything like that.'

Renko gave her a smile. 'Let's go, shall we?'

Splinters

The light moved off through the trees so quickly that even Renko and Elica had difficulty in keeping up with it. It didn't go straight either, but kept jinking, zigzagging and feinting, as if it were a football player.

'Are you all right?' Renko asked Jessica, taking her arm to help her along.

Jessica's ankle was throbbing and her left calf muscle kept going into painful spasms of cramp, but she was determined that she wasn't going to stop, and she certainly wasn't going to turn back.

They hadn't been pushing their way through the trees for more than five minutes before Jessica heard a soft, quick splintering noise off to their left.

'Did you hear that?'

'What?'

'That kind of a crackle. There it is again!'

'I don't hear anything. Come on, hurry, we're going to lose that light dude if we don't walk any faster.'

There was another splintering noise, and then another. Then Jessica heard panting – high and harsh and hungry – and she knew at once what was following them.

'It's a wooden wolf!' she gasped.

Renko looked quickly around them. 'I don't see anything. Come on, we're falling behind.'

The sound of crackling wood was coming closer and closer, and the trees on either side of them began to jostle and sway, as if something heavy were barging its way through them.

'It's a wooden wolf, Renko, I promise you.'

'*Vorbesti de lup si lupul la usã*,' panted Elica. 'When you speak of the wolf, the wolf's tail will appear.'

'Do you have a proverb for "She who is lost in a forest full of carpets should save her breath and run like fun"?'

The light was so far ahead of them now that Jessica glimpsed it only infrequently, like distant lightning. The forest grew darker and darker and the crackling sound of the wooden wolf was so loud that she felt as if it were right behind her, with its two mouths open and its hundreds of splintery teeth exposed. Even Renko turned around, and then dragged her through the trees even faster.

Suddenly the tree trunks parted with a thunderous rumble and a huge jagged shadow came bursting out at them. Out of the corner of her eye, Jessica saw a broken shape pounce on top of Elica and throw her to the ground. Elica cried out, 'Aaaahhh!' and tried to twist herself away, but the wooden wolf had taken hold of her dress and was wrenching her sideways so that it could take a bite at her throat.

Renko snatched the banister rail out of Jessica's hands, lifted it over his head and whacked the wooden wolf right behind its ear. It turned, snarling, and it was only then that Renko realized what he was up against. Four foxy eyes, two gaping jaws and a terrible heartlessness, because it was made of nothing more than shattered wood.

The wooden wolf circled around Renko, rattling deep in its oesphagus. Its claws tore at the decorative fabric of the forest floor. Renko clutched the banister rail in both hands, twisting it, weighing it up, balancing it, watching.

The light-fairy must have realized now that they weren't following, because it had stopped seven or eight trees away, its light flickering up and down like the rays from an old-fashioned movie projector.

Elica said, 'Renko—' and stepped back toward him, but as she did so something black and fluid poured out of the trees beside her. Jessica lifted her hand and warned, 'Elica – stay still. That's a shadow cat.'

More and more shadow cats emerged from the darkness. They were all different sizes and shapes – some of them sliding like oil across the forest floor, others loping through the trees like bristling hunchbacked jackals. Soon Jessica, Renko and Elica were surrounded by them, dozens of them, all of the shadows that had ever made them feel frightened all their lives. The shadow of a bedhead, or a chair, or a lampshade hanging from the ceiling.

The wooden wolf snarled and growled at Renko, but it was obviously unsettled by the sudden appearance of the shadow cats. It backed off a little way, and as it did so Renko struck its upper mouth with his banister rail. 'Get out of here!' he shouted at it. 'You're firewood, that's all you are!'

He beat the wooden wolf again and again, while the creature snarled and shook its head in rage. Fragments of oak and walnut flew in every direction. Jessica shouted, 'Renko! Be careful!' But Renko was in a frenzy, and he kept on cracking the creature's faces in a blizzard of splinters.

But then the wooden wolf took three or four steps back, crouched down, and let out a screaming roar like a circular saw tearing through a cord of timber. It reared up on its hind legs, and it was only then that Renko realized how tall it was, nearly eight feet of teeth, claws and fur-patterned veneer. He backed away, but tripped on the rumpled carpet of the forest floor, and the wooden wolf literally collapsed over him, both of its jaws gaping.

At the last second, Renko rolled sideways, so that the wooden wolf crashed down right beside him. As it twisted its head around, trying to bite at his arms, he pushed one end of the banister rail into its lower mouth, and forced the other end into its upper mouth, so that both of its jaws were wedged wide open.

The beast screeched even more furiously, but not in triumph this time. It rolled over onto its back, its legs thrashing, shaking its head wildly from side to side. It was then that the shadow cats went for it. The light-fairy was quickly coming back, and already Jessica and Elica were too brightly lit for the shadow cats to attack them. But the wooden wolf was still struggling helplessly in the darkness, and the shadow cats preferred to go for a helpless prey.

As it rolled over again, three of the bristling shadow cats leaped onto the wolf's back, while one of the oily, slug-like ones slid right into its wide-open mouth, followed by another and then another.

The light-fairy came back around the last few trees, and suddenly the forest was lit up like a stage-set. 'Hurry,' it urged. 'We don't have any more time to waste.'

'Renko!' called Jessica. Renko climbed to his feet and came after them, brushing the splinters of wood from his sleeves.

Elica turned and looked back at the wooden wolf, still snarling and writhing from side to side, almost completely buried in the black shapes of the shadow cats.

'What will they do to it?' she asked.

'They will do what shadows always do,' answered the light-fairy. 'They will tear it to pieces, and swallow it in darkness forever.'

The light-fairy started to glide back in the direction from which it had come, and the teenagers followed it. But they had hardly covered twenty feet before they heard a hideous scream – a scream of pain, despair, utter terror. The wooden wolf exploded into hundreds of chunks of wood, and the shadow cats pounced on its remains. Although Jessica knew that the creature had only been made of walnut and oak, she was still sickened by the greedy crunching noises that the shadow cats made as they devoured it.

'Please, hurry,' said the light-fairy. 'We are nearly through the forest now, but we still have to get to the house. It could be too late already.'

House of Mirrors

A fter five or ten minutes Jessica began to see twilight through the trees, and soon they were out in the open, climbing a hill that was covered with fine purplish grasses. The air was fresh and chilly, and the stars were beginning to come out, one by one, like the streetlights in a very distant city.

The light-fairy circled around them, and it was obvious now that its electrical charge was beginning to fail. 'There is nothing more I can do for you now. You must carry on by yourselves, if you are still set on saving those children.'

'Thank you,' said Jessica. 'We couldn't have come this far without you.'

'You may not have cause to thank me when you encounter the Stain.'

'We'll be all right,' Renko assured it. 'If we can whup a wooden wolf I don't think there's much that any old stain can do.'

'Be fearful,' said the light-fairy. 'The Stain can drain away all life as you know it.'

The light-fairy circled once more, then drifted off toward the east, its light dwindling as it went. In less than a minute it had disappeared altogether, and they were left on the hillside by themselves.

They carried on. On the horizon they could make out the steely shine of the ocean, with the moon reflected in it. The hill gradually descended, and they saw trees silhouetted

against the sky like black lace, but so far there was no sign
at all of a house.

'Maybe we make mistake,' said Elica. 'Maybe we should
go back.'

'We've come too far now,' Jessica told her, although
she was beginning to feel frightened too. Her ankle was
throbbing painfully and her hip hurt from limping. Renko
tried to support her, but the ground was too uneven and
most of the time he ended up making it even more difficult
for her to walk.

'There is no house,' said Elica, and there was panic in her
voice. 'Where is the house? If we cannot find house—'

'Hold on,' Renko interrupted her. 'There's some people
walking toward us. Look – down there!'

They stopped and strained their eyes. Renko was right.
There were three figures standing in a clearing beside the
trees. Renko waved and shouted, 'Hello! Are you the
Pennington kids? Hello!'

One of the figures waved back, but that was all.

'You'd think they'd make the effort and, like, meet us
halfway,' Renko complained.

They carried on walking. It looked as if the three figures
had taken the hint, because they carried on walking too.
Jessica waved both arms and one of the figures waved both
arms back at her.

Renko stopped again. They all stopped, and the figures
stopped too.

'That's not the Pennington kids,' said Renko, in exaspera-
tion. 'That's us.'

'Then this must be the house,' said Jessica. 'When the
angel said "house of mirrors", I thought she meant it was like
one of those carnival houses, with loads of funny mirrors in
it. But it's all mirrors. Look – you can just about see it now.
The walls, the chimneys, the windows. It's all mirrors.'

They started walking toward the house as fast as they

could, and the figures in the house began to hurry too. Because it was twilight it was almost impossible to tell where the house ended and where the sky began, but as they came nearer its outline became clearer – a small two-story building with a verandah and a mansard roof. It shone like a mirage, a mirage with black reflected trees and violet reflected grass and twinkling reflected stars, but it was real. There was even a garden around it, with crazy-paving pathways made out of fragments of mirror, and crushed green bottle-glass instead of grass.

Jessica climbed the steps to the front door, and that was a mirror too. She could see herself standing on the verandah with one hand raised to knock, and Renko and Elica right behind her. There was a knocker hanging in the middle of the door that looked like a circular hand-mirror, with a face engraved on the glass, a woman's face with sightless eyes and a single tear on her cheek.

Jessica had already raised the knocker when the door clicked open. A small voice whispered, 'Who is it? Who's there?'

'Phoebe? It's us – Jessica and Renko and Elica. We've come to save you.'

'It's too late. The Stain's coming.'

'We know that, Phoebe, and that's why we really have to hurry.'

'We'll all die if we go back through the wallpaper.'

'No, you won't. I went to the doctor. There's a cure for spotted fever. He can make you all well again.'

'Papa made us promise not to leave until there's a cure.'

'There *is* a cure, I promise you. Why would I lie?'

Phoebe opened the door wider. She looked white and tired and her cheeks were blotchy. She was wearing a short blue dress with white polka dots on it, with a bow at the back, and very worn-out black sandals.

'You'd better come in.'

Jessica stepped inside. The interior of the house was the same as the outside, with everything mirrored – the walls, the ceiling, the floors, even the stairs and the stair rails. There were fingerprints all over the mirrors, all the way up the stairs, like flocks of ghostly butterflies. Jessica could faintly smell antiseptic, and something that reminded her of lilac.

There was an umbrella-stand in the hallway, and when Jessica looked into one of the side rooms she could see armchairs and couches. They were heavy 1930s-style, and all upholstered in brown diamond patterns. There was only one picture on the mirrored walls, the black-and-white photograph of a stern-looking man in a suit, with his hand on the shoulder of a sad, wide-eyed woman.

'Where are your brothers and sisters?' Jessica asked Phoebe. 'You're not alone here, are you?'

'They're all upstairs. They're not very well. They're never very well, none of us is.'

'Well, let's go up and see them, shall we? We need to get out of here as soon as we can.'

'Tickity-tock, tickity-tock,' said Phoebe.

Jessica put her arm around her shoulders and said, 'You've been here such a long time, Phoebe, feeling ill all the time. Come on, we're going to get you out of here.'

'Is my mommy still alive?' asked Phoebe, looking up at her. For the first time Jessica noticed that she had a smattering of cinnamon-colored freckles across the bridge of her nose.

'No, Phoebe, she's not. It's been such a long time. Years and years and years, but living here, you haven't ever noticed.'

'My mommy's really dead?'

Renko glanced at her, but Jessica said, 'I'm afraid so. I'm sorry. And your daddy too.'

Phoebe looked one way and then the other, as if she

couldn't decide what to do. Jessica said, 'If it helps, sweet-heart, I lost both of my parents too, not more than a year ago, in an automobile accident. You can learn to handle it. You can. So many people will help you, me included. And Renko. And Elica.'

Phoebe stood for a moment at the foot of the mirrored stairs, bowed her head and covered her eyes with her hand. Renko tapped the dial of his wristwatch to indicate that they should get moving, but two large tears were sliding down Phoebe's cheeks and Jessica waved her hand to say, Give her a moment, allow her just a moment of grief. She had probably always realized that her parents must be dead, but this was the first time that anybody had confirmed it, somebody who knew for sure.

After a minute, Phoebe smeared her eyes with her fingers. 'All right. I'll take you up to see the rest of them.'

They climbed the mirrored stairs, and sometimes there were four of them, and sometimes eight, and sometimes thirty-two, depending on the mirrors they were looking at. At the top of the stairs, there were three mirrors at an angle, and hundreds of reflected images of all of them went curving off into infinity.

Phoebe said, 'Have you ever wondered what it's like in there?'

'In where?' asked Jessica.

'In there, in the mirror? Does it go all the way round, in a circle?'

'I don't know.'

'I think about it,' said Phoebe. 'It frightens me. I can see all those mes. Which me is the real me? I mean, if I leave here now, will I have to leave all the other mes behind?'

'You don't have to be frightened of anything,' Jessica told her. 'And the real you is you. None of those reflections would move or smile or wave or do anything unless you did.'

Phoebe took Jessica's hand and led her into a mirrored bedroom. Two plain old-fashioned iron beds stood side by side, and on each bed sat a boy. They had cropped 1940s haircuts, with protruding ears, and they both looked very thin and pale, with the same crimson blotches on their cheeks as Phoebe. They both wore big flappy sport coats and gray flannel pants.

'This is Martin,' said Phoebe, tugging Jessica's hand and leading her toward the taller of the two boys. Martin was lanky, with sensitive brown eyes and thick brown eyebrows, and Jessica could see that he took after his mother.

'Martin, these are the people I told you about,' said Phoebe. 'They said that Daddy and Mommy are dead.'

'I know they're dead,' said Martin, quietly. 'They would have come for us, wouldn't they, if they weren't?'

'Hi, Martin,' said Renko. 'Listen, we kind of know what's happened to you, how you got stuck in this wallpaper situation and all. We came here to take you back to the real world, right?'

'Is there a cure?' asked the younger boy, sharply. He looked more like his father, with wide-spaced eyes and a turned-up nose.

'This is David,' said Phoebe proudly, sitting beside him on the bed and taking hold of his hand. 'David's eleven next birthday, aren't you, David?'

'Is there a cure?' David repeated, aggressively.

'Yes,' said Jessica. 'There is a cure. It's called doxycycline and it was invented just after your parents stopped coming to see you. They never would have known about it. They did their best.'

David said, 'I hope you're not lying to us, because if you're lying to us—'

Jessica pointed a finger at him. 'Listen – you called out to me and I heard you and I came to save your life.'

David said, 'My mom said she would come to take care

of us. Then my dad said that everything was all right. And what happened? Nothing. They never came back. And that was a whole week ago. Or maybe it wasn't a week ago. Maybe it was longer. I don't know. A month?'

Jessica reached out and took hold of his hand. 'David, it was fifty-two years.'

'I knew it was fifty-two years,' said Martin. 'I told you it was fifty-two years. That's why the Stain is starting to leak out.'

David looked into her eyes, and even though his mouth was shaping itself up all ready to deny it, she could tell that, in his soul, he believed her.

'Fifty-two years?' he asked her.

'Yes. We have to go. And I mean we have to go now.'

'I'll wake up Maggie and Joel.'

'Thank you, David. Really.'

He pried her hand away from his shoulder. 'You don't have to thank me. If it wasn't for the Stain, none of us would want to go back.'

'But none of this is real, is it? You're living inside a wallpaper pattern!'

'Of course it's real. You can see it, can't you? You can feel it!'

'Please – call the rest of them,' said Jessica. 'We have to get out of here as soon as we can.'

David was about to start arguing again, but Martin turned to him and said, 'That's enough, David. Let's get everybody ready to go.'

Without any warning at all, tears began to run down David's blotchy cheeks.

Night of the Stain

In a smaller bedroom upstairs, surrounded by dozens of mirrors, in a silver-painted cot with tattered lace curtains, they found little Joel, no more than three years old. He was flushed and feverish like his brothers and sisters, but he was quiet and almost surreally calm. Jessica lifted him out of his cot and stroked his sticky blond hair. He stared up at her with his pale blue eyes as she changed him out of his teddy-bear pajamas and dressed him up in a brown corduroy romper suit with a fur-lined hood.

'It's going to be cold outside, Joel. Don't worry. Jessica's going to take care of you.'

Renko came to the nursery door. 'It's almost dark outside. I hope we know what we're doing.'

'We didn't have any choice, did we? We know that Dr Leeming can cure them. We couldn't just leave them here.'

'But the Stain – I've been out on the verandah. I can hear noises already coming from the east, and they don't sound good.'

'What kind of noises?'

Renko shrugged. 'Crushing, and crying. I don't know. It sounds like somebody mincing up live babies.'

'Renko, in case anything horrible happens, I just want you to know how glad I am that you came with us.'

Renko, embarrassed, scruffed one hand through his hair. 'Of course I came. I like you.'

'You do?'

'Is that such a surprise?'

'But—'

'But what? You hurt your ankle in a car crash? You draw fairies and elves all the time, and you dress like somebody's granny? Do you think that's going to put me off?'

Jessica finished buttoning Joel's corduroy suit. 'No,' she said, without looking up. 'Now that I know you, I don't suppose it is.'

They found Margaret in another small room at the back of the house. Margaret was twelve, and just like Martin she was a haunting image of her mother – thin, with long, dark, braided hair and dreamy brown eyes. She had tried to make her mirrored room prettier by winding strips of lace and dried flowers around the railings of her iron bed, and hanging fishing-nets at the window in place of curtains, all decorated with ribbons, bows and silver-paper stars.

She sat up at once when David shook her shoulder. 'What is it? What's happened? Is it the Stain?'

'We have to leave,' said Jessica. 'Get dressed as quickly as you can. It won't be long before the Stain takes over everything.'

'Where are we going to go?' she asked hoarsely.

'Back to the real world,' Renko told her. 'You don't have to stay here any longer.'

She stood up. She was wearing a white ankle-length nightdress with puffy sleeves and a smocked bodice. Jessica noticed that she was wearing a thin gold chain around her neck, from which a sapphire ring was dangling.

'That ring – is that your grandmother's?'

Margaret clasped is tightly in her hand and nodded. 'My mother gave it to me. She said that one day I would be able to give it back to my grandmother. But I don't see how I ever can.'

Jessica looked quickly at Renko. Time was passing faster

and faster, and this wasn't the moment to tell Margaret that her grandmother had been torn to shreds by shadow cats.

Within ten minutes all of the Pennington children were dressed in tweed coats, woolly hats and gloves and had assembled in the mirrored hallway. It looked as if there were a hundred of them, rather than eight.

'I guess you're all going to miss living here,' Jessica said to Martin.

He nodded. 'It was kind of a comfort, you know, always being able to see yourself, and what you were doing; and your brothers and sisters, too. It was kind of like living in a movie of your own life. But at least we never felt alone. See?' he said, raising his arm, and twenty other Martins raised their arms to him in greeting. 'We always had our own reflections.'

'Is that why your parents built this place?'

'I guess so, partly. But mostly because it's difficult to find, difficult for any pattern creatures to see – you know, like wooden wolves or cloud dogs or shadow cats.' He paused, and then he said, 'They did their best to look after us, didn't they, my dad and mom?'

Jessica said, 'Yes, they did. You're going to find it very different, when you get back. Things have changed a whole lot since your parents first took you through the wall.'

'We'll cope, don't you worry. We've managed to take care of ourselves for over fifty-two years, haven't we?'

Renko opened the front door. 'Look, it's real dark now. We'd better hustle.'

They hurried down the steps and out across the garden of crushed-up glass. Low black clouds had rolled in from the east, so that the sky was almost completely covered except for a few stray stars on the western horizon. The temperature had fallen, too, so that their breath smoked as they made their way through the gate and started to climb back up the hill toward the forest of carpets.

Jessica paused for a moment to listen. Renko was right: underneath the fluffing of the wind, she could hear a low grinding sound, like some huge machine whose purpose could only be guessed at; and in counterpoint to the grinding, an occasional high-pitched scream. As yet the sound was too far away for her to be able to tell if they were human screams, or if they were simply the screeching of cogs and gears. But there was no question that it was growing steadily louder, and so whatever was causing it was coming closer.

'That's the Stain,' Martin told her.

'How do you know?'

'The Light People always told us that when the Stain leaked out it would sound like a factory for swallowing up the whole world.'

They continued their climb up the hill. The five Pennington children all held hands, with Joel and Phoebe in the middle, so that they formed a chain, like the Von Trapp children in *The Sound of Music*. Jessica found it unexpectedly touching and sad. Respecting their family closeness, she and Renko and Elica followed a little way behind.

'How are we finding our way back through the trees?' asked Elica, out of breath.

David heard her, and turned his head. 'Just follow me, I know the forest like the back of my hand.'

Martin turned around too. 'Not only that, he has a long cord which runs all the way through the forest from one side to the other.'

When they reached the crest of the hill they looked back at the house of mirrors where the Pennington children had lived for so many years. It was almost invisible in the encroaching darkness, only the faintest of gleams.

'It seems like only yesterday that Daddy and Mommy brought us here,' said Phoebe, in a wistful voice.

'In a way, it was,' Jessica told her.

'What did you eat?' asked Elica. 'How did you live?'

'We were ill . . . we never had any appetite.'

'In fifty-two years?' said Renko.

'Time's different here,' Jessica reminded him.

As they looked down at the house of mirrors, they heard the grinding of the Stain grow distinctly louder. Below them, from the east, a blackness was spreading across the grasslands, a blackness even darker than the clouds above. It advanced like a tide of volcanic lava, except that it didn't glow at all, and they could smell its coldness on the wind, and a terrible stench of rotting flesh.

The Stain reached the garden wall and poured thickly over it. Even from here, on top of the hill, they could hear glass breaking. Within less than a minute, the house of mirrors had been completely demolished, its mansard roof collapsing inward, its shining walls shattered, and what was left of it was carried along in the awful flow of putrescence.

Jessica had never physically felt evil before, not like this. The relentless sliding of the Stain across the countryside made her mouth go dry, and she seriously began to think that they might not be able to escape it.

'Here's David's trusty cord,' said Martin. It was a length of green brocade, exactly the same pattern as the brocade that ran around the edges of Grannie's best furniture, and it had been knotted at intervals to form a guideline that would show them the way through the forest.

'Come on,' said David, taking hold of the cord. 'Quick as you can but don't let go. You can get lost in these trees before you know it.'

'He's speaking from experience,' put in Martin. 'He got lost so many times, and every time we had to call the Light People to rescue him.'

'I could easily have found my way out on my own,' David protested.

'Of course you could,' said Margaret. 'That's why you gave Martin your best penknife, because you were so grateful to him for finding you.'

'That was a present, that's all.'

'Tickity-tock, tickity-tock,' warned Phoebe.

It seemed to take them hours to make their way through the forest, and Jessica was beginning to panic. The tree-curtains were dusty and oppressive, and there seemed to be more and more of them, all swaying and swinging around her so that she could hardly breathe.

At last, however, they burst out of the trees and into the chilly night air. In front of them lay the painted lake, but it was now so dark that they couldn't see the opposite shore. They stopped when they reached the water's edge and listened again, and this time the grinding noise of the Stain was very distinct. There was no question about it, too: the screams weren't the sound of gear-wheels clashing together, they were humans and animals.

'Where's it coming from?' asked Renko.

'Over there, I think,' said Martin, pointing toward the north-east. 'If we cross the lake to that side there, where the fishing-boats are tied up, we should be all right.'

Joel sneezed and said, 'I'm cold, Phoebe. I want to go back to bed.'

Jessica knelt down beside him. 'You can't go back to bed, darling, I'm sorry. Your house is all gone.'

'Where?'

'It's gone to house heaven, where all the good houses go. I expect angels will live in it now.'

'I want it to come back.'

'I know. But we all have to be brave, and keep on walking as fast as we can.'

They crossed the waters of the painted lake like Polish refugees crossing the frozen Vistula, and even if the water had been real, it was now so cold that it probably would have been solid ice. All five of the Pennington children started to cough, especially Margaret, and this reminded Jessica how sick they were, and how close to death, no matter what happened to them.

All the time the noise of the Stain grew louder and nearer, and they could hear now that it wasn't only grinding and screaming, but a deep ripping sound, as if the very fabric of the world were being torn up; and a brassy discordant trumpeting; and a squealing like a thousand knives on a thousand dinner plates.

Phoebe clamped her hands over her ears, and Joel began to sob in fright. All eight of them were now running as fast as they could, with Renko gripping Jessica's arm to stop her from tripping.

They were not much more than halfway across when Renko swore, and stopped.

'What is it?' asked Jessica, and the others stopped too.

'Look,' said Renko. All across one corner of the painted lake, crawling toward them over its surface, was a writhing black mass. It was impossible to see exactly what it consisted of, but every now and then Jessica could see hideous shapes emerging from it and then sinking back down again, and for an instant she thought she saw arms waving, and then something that looked like a skeletal bull.

'We're not going to make it, are we?' said Martin.

'We have to make it,' said Jessica.

'But it's going to cut us off before we can reach the shore.'

Already the Stain had reached the horse and cart that stood axle-deep in the painted water. Without stopping, it picked them up and carried them off, dipping and swirling, as if they had fallen into a slow-motion flood. The painted horse was stiffly carried away, making no more protest than a carousel horse, but Jessica could hear the tortured screams of other animals inside the ever-advancing torrent, and a woman pleading for her life, and a man screaming in agony.

'It floated!' she said.

'What? What are you talking about?'

'The cart! It floated!'

'So what does that mean?'

'We can reach the fishing-boats before the Stain gets there! We can float on the Stain and row our way to the shore!'

'Those boats, they're not even real! They're painted!'

'It doesn't matter! If the cart floated the boats will float!'

'We should go back, it's our only chance.'

'You saw the Stain take over your house, and all the fields around it. We can't go back.'

Martin turned to Renko, and then to David, and said, 'What do you think?'

Jessica said, 'I think we should vote on it. Who's for going back and who's for going forward? Put your hands up, all those who want to go forward.'

Phoebe immediately put her hand up; so did Joel. Margaret hesitated for a while, and then she did too. Martin followed, saying, 'Why not? What have we got to lose?' Renko raised his hand, with Elica's.

In the end, David said, 'All right. But if it all goes wrong, and we all get killed, don't blame me.'

They jogged across the paint-crusted water until they reached the fishing-boats. The boats smelled strongly of fish and tar, and there were oars and tackle and nets in them. The Pennington children climbed into the nearest boat, which was just big enough for the five of them, while Jessica, Renko and Elica climbed into the boat moored next to it. Unlike real boats, they didn't dip or sway, and they sat in them completely motionless, under a sky as black as squid-ink.

'What do we now?' called Martin.

Jessica called back, 'Wait until the Stain reaches us, and then pick up the oars and row!'

Joel began to sob even more loudly, and Phoebe put her arm around him to comfort him. Jessica thought: If I die now, at least I'll get to see Dad and Mom again. But please don't let me die now. And don't let little Joel die, or Phoebe, or Margaret or David or Martin. They've been waiting so long for somebody to save them.

Renko reached out and took hold of Jessica's hand. He didn't say anything but he had a look in his eye, a look which said, If we don't come out of this, if we're all killed, I want you to know how much I care about you. And she gave him a tight, frightened smile, and touched his cheek, prickly like a gooseberry with his first stubble, and she could have kissed him, but she didn't.

It was then that the Stain arrived, with a thunderous undertone and a deafening screech. It was like a huge viscid wave of black molasses, crammed with stinking garbage and half-decayed bodies. Jessica squeezed her eyes tight shut as the Stain poured underneath the fishing-boats, but she couldn't stop herself from opening them up again, and all she could see was frantically waving skeletons, and cats with no hair, and giraffes with their necks half eaten by sharks. Things rose out of the Stain that even the foulest mind on earth couldn't imagine: rotting babies impaled on fence posts, crows with no legs, men with their faces eaten away by acid and leprosy. They swirled and bobbed around the fishing-boats, and some of them were screaming, but others were terribly silent.

'Oh God,' said Renko; and it was then that the Stain lifted up the first painted fishing-boat, with the Pennington children in it, so that it reared and rotated. Joel let out a high-pitched shriek of terror, but Phoebe held him tight, and David held Phoebe.

The next thing they knew, their own boat bucked up beneath them, and they had to cling on to the gunwales to stop themselves from being flung out into the Stain. They dipped and turned around 360 degrees, with all the monstrosities screaming at them from every side. A fleshless elephant came thundering out of the Stain right next to them, with filthy rags and seaweed dripping from its tusks, and let out an agonized cry that sounded like the death of all elephants everywhere.

'Row!' screamed Jessica. 'Row!'

Renko picked up the painted oars and maneuvered them into the rowlocks. His hair was sticking up and his face was white with fear, but he managed to thrust the oars into the Stain and pull, and pull again, and turn the fishing-boat around until they were heading toward the shore. A fork of lightning lit up the painted lake, so that they could see Martin and Margaret rowing for the shore too. Then they were deafened by bellowing thunder, and it began to rain, torrentially.

It seemed to take them forever to row to the shore, and sometimes it seemed as if the Stain were actually sucking them backward. They were too frightened to scream or cry any more, and they were devoting too much of their strength to rowing. The rain crashed down on them as if the heavens were determined to fill up their boats with water and sink them.

Jessica saw a headless sow float past, her piglets still desperately trying to feed from her. She saw scores of struggling cats whose tails had all been knotted together. She saw a woman, still alive but lying motionless in all of that filth, stunned into stary-eyed paralysis by the horror that was engulfing her.

Renko heaved at the oars again and again, pulling so hard that he was almost standing up. There was an appalling gurgling noise, and the boat's prow dipped beneath the surface. Jessica was convinced that they were going to go under, but Renko gave another heave, and they were suddenly washed toward the shore.

The boat turned around, and tipped, and Jessica heard the grating of soil underneath the keel.

'We've made it!' Renko shouted. 'Everybody out, as fast as you can!'

They clambered out of the boat, splashing knee-deep in oily black sludge. Lightning flashed again, and yet again, and Jessica could see that the Pennington children had reached the shore too, and that Martin was giving Joel a piggy-back away from the boat.

Gasping, they all hurried away from the painted lake and up the hill toward the garden where Mrs Crawford was waiting for them with Epiphany. They went through the hedges and Mrs Crawford was still there, kneeling on the grass with Epiphany's head in her lap.

'That didn't take you long,' she said, in relief.

'We've been hours,' said Jessica, kneeling down beside her.

'Not at all . . . you've only been away for twenty minutes, if that.'

'Did you try going back through the wallpaper? Are the phones working yet?'

'I went once, but they're not working yet. Epiphany's still breathing, but her pulse is very weak. I don't think we can take her back until we're sure that we can call for an ambulance.'

'But the Stain is coming . . . we only just managed to get away from it. And if you think we've only been away for twenty minutes, it could be here before we know it.'

'Get these children through the wallpaper,' said Mrs Crawford. 'I'll wait here with Epiphany for as long as I can.'

'I can't leave you here,' said Jessica. 'I can't leave Piff, either.'

'If you take her back and you can't get an ambulance for her, she's going to die.'

'I can't leave her! What am I going to do?'

It was then that the stone angel said, 'You were told before, Jessica. You have to wash away the Stain.'

'How can I wash it away? There's much too much of it!'

'Where do you think this land came from? These trees, these hills?'

'The pattern on my bedroom wallpaper. What does that have to do with it?'

'So where do you think the Stain came from?'

Jessica stared at the angel, and suddenly she realized what it was trying to tell her. 'The Stain came from my wallpaper too. There's a stain on my wallpaper, that's what caused it, and all I have to do is wash it off!'

'Go, then,' said the angel, with a gentle smile. 'Go as quick as you can, and you can still save your friend.'

Jessica stood up. As she did so, however, Renko laid a hand on her shoulder.

'Look,' he said. 'I think we're too late.'

Between the cemetery and the overgrown garden which led to the wallpaper, a thick black tide was already pouring across the grass, a tide that carried sickening carcasses, tangled ribcages and heaps of stinking, hairy slime.

'It's the Stain,' Jessica told Mrs Crawford. 'It's cut us off.'

Screams in the Dark

'What can we do now?' asked Elica. 'We can only pray.'

'Can't we wade through it?' said Martin.

'I'll go,' David volunteered. 'It's only muck, isn't it? I put my hand down the toilet once, when I dropped my watch.'

'The Stain will drag you down and drown you,' said the stone angel. 'It is deeper and darker than the worst deed that any man can commit.'

'Then what can we do?' asked Jessica.

'We're all going to die,' said Phoebe. 'I knew we would, as sure as clocks are clocks. Tickity-tock, tickity-tock!'

Mrs Crawford stood up and said, 'I'll have a try. I've already had a very long life.'

'No!' Jessica protested. 'You heard what the angel said: you'll be dragged down and drowned, and all for nothing!'

'There is one way,' said the stone angel. 'Every statue has a gift – a gift that was given by whoever carved it. If a statue so wishes, it can move, just once, but *only* once. Many statues never use that gift; they prefer to stay still forever, happy in the knowledge that they could move if they wanted to. Some statues give their gift to people who need it more than they do. That's why disabled people touch the statues of saints, in the hope that they can walk again.'

'I don't know what you're trying to say,' Jessica interrupted impatiently. 'Look, the Stain's pouring into the garden!'

171

Joel started to cry again, and Margaret picked him up, but Jessica could see by the expression on her face that she was just as frightened as her baby brother. A crackling fork of lightning hit a nearby tree and set its branches alight, like a terrible candelabrum, and then the sky was split by a deafening rumble of thunder.

'I have a gift which all angels have,' said the stone angel. 'I can fly . . . just once, if I want to. Or else I can give that gift to somebody else. To you, Jessica, so that you can cross the Stain and reach your wallpaper again.'

'What?' said Jessica, in disbelief.

'Come here,' said the stone angel. 'Stand in front of me, and let me fold my wings around you.'

'I won't be able to fly,' said Jessica.

'How many things have you seen here that you didn't think possible? Did you think that roses could talk to you, or that your wardrobe could try to eat you alive? Come here, child, there isn't much time.'

'Go on, Jess,' Renko urged her. 'What else are we going to do?'

Jessica felt a brief warm surge of happiness that Renko had given her a nickname. Jess. Hesitantly, Jessica walked up to the angel and stood in front of it. The Stain was pouring thickly into the cemetery now, between the gravestones, and there were screams and groans and sickly wallowing noises.

The angel smiled down at Jessica so blindly and sweetly that Jessica felt a lump in her throat. Then it folded its wide wings around her and embraced her, and even though its wings were carved from stone she felt as if they were real feathers, soft and gray, and that here in the angel's embrace she was as close to heaven as she would ever get while she was alive.

'Now,' said the angel, and took its wings away. Jessica turned, and all of the others were looking at her expectantly.

'I don't know what to do,' said Jessica, in desperation. 'Do I flap my arms? What?'

'My darling, you just fly,' said the angel.

Jessica slowly extended her arms, as wide as she could, and it was then that she felt the most extraordinary fizzing sensation passing through her, from her head to her toes. At the same time, she literally shone, like one of the Light People, and she could see her light illuminate the faces of all the Pennington children, and Renko, Elica and Mrs Crawford, as if they were witnessing a miracle.

Which, in a way, they were. Jessica rose silently from the grass, with her arms still outstretched, and glided over the cemetery gardens, over the Stain, a golden kite without a string. She flew toward the overgrown garden, and without stopping she flew straight toward the wallpaper pattern. She squeezed her eyes tight shut and when she opened them again she was standing in her bedroom.

Immediately, frantically, she started searching for the stain. It wasn't behind the curtains. It wasn't behind her dressing-table mirror. She dragged out the closet and shone her flashlight behind it, but it wasn't there, either.

'Please, please, please,' she repeated. She knew that the others had only a few minutes left before they were all engulfed.

She pulled out her bed and looked behind the bedhead – and there, at last, she saw it: a wide brown stain in the shape of a pig's head, but she knew that it wasn't really a pig's head. It was Mrs Pennington's blood, from the evening fifty-two years ago when her husband had stabbed her to death and left her looking as if she had been daubed all over with red paint.

Jessica opened her bedroom door and ran downstairs. Grace was in the kitchen, polishing the range. 'You children back already?' she said. 'Where's Epiphany? Upstairs? You tell that girl to come down here and start her homework!'

Without saying a word, Jessica hurtled into the scullery, picked up a zinc pail and noisily filled it with hot water. 'What you doing there, Jessica?' Grace wanted to know. 'If there's anything needs cleaning up, I can do it!'

Jessica opened the cupboard under the sink and found a scrubbing brush and a pack of scouring-powder. She limped through the kitchen and back upstairs, leaving Grace standing by the range shaking her head. 'You just tell Epiphany to come down and make a start on her math!'

Back in her bedroom, Jessica pushed her bed further away from the wall and sloshed half the hot water onto the wallpaper. Then she sprinkled scouring powder on the brush and began to scrub at the stain as hard as she could.

'Jessica!' cried a voice. It was Mrs Crawford. 'Jessica, can you hear us? You have to hurry!'

'The Stain's almost here!' shouted Renko. 'Please, Jessica! Faster!'

Jessica scrubbed at the wallpaper, holding the brush in both hands, but the stain was so old that she couldn't make any impression on it. As she scrubbed, however, a small ribbon of damp wallpaper was rucked up and torn away, then another. She dropped the brush and began to tear the paper away from the wall, until the stain was completely ripped away. She crumpled up the stained wallpaper, opened the bedroom window and threw it out into the snow.

'I've done it!' she shouted. 'I've got rid of it!'

She listened, but there was no answer.

'It's gone!' she called. 'I tore it off and threw it out of the window!'

Still no reply.

She didn't know if she ought to go back through the wallpaper. She was frightened of what she might see, and what might happen to her if the Stain had taken over everything. But she couldn't leave Renko and Elica and Epiphany behind, nor Mrs Crawford, nor the Pennington children.

She hesitated for a moment, and as she hesitated she heard the phone ringing in the hallway downstairs. The lines must have been repaired, which meant that she could phone for an ambulance for Piff. That decided her. She jumped up onto her bed and threw herself through the wallpaper.

At once, Jessica was almost blinded by lightning, and deafened by the most hideous roaring and screaming she had ever heard. Rain was lashing onto the overgrown garden, beating down the rose-bushes and flattening the grass. In an instant she was soaked, and her hair was plastered to her face.

Lightning struck again and again, walking across the clouds like fiery stilts, so that it was hard to see what was happening. But as she struggled across the overgrown garden, one hand lifted to protect her face from the rain, she saw that the Stain looked as if it were boiling. Great gouts of oily black liquid were jumping into the air, and bits and pieces of bones and bodies were jumping up with them.

Jessica saw a headless skeleton spring up and perform a jerky, broken dance before scattering back into the Stain in disassembled pieces. Something that looked like a rotting dolphin was thrown up too, in a ghastly parody of a live dolphin leaping through the sea.

But, for all its screaming and grinding and furious boiling, the Stain was crawling away. It had already drawn back from the hedges around the cemetery, and as Jessica made her way back across the grass she saw that it was ebbing faster and faster. It had left the ground covered in greasy, stinking slime, but she knew that she had washed it away.

She reached the cemetery. The Pennington children were clustered close together, holding each other's hands, and although they looked so pale they were clearly relieved. Mrs Crawford was stroking Epiphany's forehead and Renko was kneeling beside her too, feeling her pulse.

Elica said, 'You are the bravest. You have said to the

Stain, out!' And she came up and put her arms around Jessica and held her tight.

Jessica said, 'The phones are working again . . . we can take Piff back. And we can call Dr Leeming, too, to bring five doses of doxycycline.'

Renko stood up. 'You did it, Jessica. You beat it. We're all real proud of you. I mean it.'

There was a last grumble of thunder and the skies began to clear. It was morning again, and the sun was shining. High above them they saw a V-shaped formation of nutcrackers, flying who could only guess where.

'Come on,' said Mrs Crawford, 'let's be as quick as we can.' She picked up one corner of her raincoat, while Renko, Martin and David took hold of the others. Led by Phoebe and Joel, they left the cemetery and began to walk toward the overgrown garden.

Jessica turned and looked at the stone angel, its wings still wet with rain.

'Go along,' said the angel. 'Your future's waiting for you.'

'I'll come back,' Jessica promised.

'I don't think you'll ever need to. What you have done here – the things that you have seen and experienced – they will stand you in good stead for the rest of your life.'

'Goodbye,' said Jessica, and followed the others toward the wallpaper pattern. Mrs Crawford had already carried Epiphany through, and only Margaret was left.

She never knew if it was a freak accident, or if the Stain were capable of wreaking its revenge, but as she came up to Margaret there was a devastating crack of lightning, and she was flung, stunned, toward the wallpaper.

Waking

S he opened her eyes. The sun was shining in bars across
the ceiling, and it was so bright that she could hardly
look at it. Her head was throbbing and her mouth felt as if
somebody had spooned sand into it.

Dr Leeming leaned over her bed, the sunlight gleaming
on his bald head. 'Good, you're awake. How are you
feeling?'

'I don't know.' She tried to lift her head from the pillow
and look around. There was a jug of water next to her bed
with bubbles in it, and a vase of red chrysanthemums.
'Where am I?'

'You're in hospital. You had a very nasty fall at school.
Banged your head.'

'School? How long have I been here?'

'Since yesterday afternoon.'

'Where's Epiphany? Did you manage to save Epiphany?'

Dr Leeming blinked at her. 'Epiphany Russell? Grace
Russell's girl?'

'That's right. Did you manage to get her to hospital?'

'Why would Epiphany need to go to hospital?'

'She was knocked over by a car . . . she was dying.'

Dr Leeming smiled and shook his head. 'I think I would
have heard about it if she had been.'

'What about Renko and Elica and the Pennington children?'

'I think your brain must have been making up stories. That often happens when you suffer a severe concussion.'

'No, I couldn't have made it up. I couldn't.'

Dr Leeming said, 'What sometimes happens is, little subconscious anxieties get blown up into quite believable dramas. It's the same mechanism as dreaming, except that the patient is totally convinced that these dramas really happened.'

Jessica lay back; she couldn't think what to say. She had gone through the wallpaper, she knew she had. Telling her that it was nothing but 'quite believable dramas' was ridiculous, like telling her that her whole life had been nothing but a 'quite believable drama'.

'Listen,' said Dr Leeming. 'You get yourself some sleep and I'll go call your grandparents and tell them you've come round. They've been very worried about you. Would you like anything to drink? Coke, maybe?'

Jessica whispered, 'No . . . no, thank you.'

After Dr Leeming had left she lay and stared at the ceiling and quite unexpectedly she began to cry.

She left hospital the following afternoon at three o'clock. It was much gloomier outside, and it was snowing again.

'You're quiet,' remarked Grandpa Willy as he walked along the corridor with her.

'It's going to take Jessica a few days to readjust,' Dr Leeming explained. 'Bring her in to see me again on Monday, so that I can make sure she's OK.'

Halfway along the corridor, a door opened and a nurse came out, smiling at Dr Leeming as she did so. Jessica glanced into the room, where a very pale young girl was lying in bed watching television. With a jolt, she saw that it was Phoebe.

She stopped, and Grandpa Willy said, 'What is it, Jessica? Are you OK?'

'That little girl – who is she?'

'We don't know her name,' said Dr Leeming. 'That's one of the kids who were found wandering around near Allen's Corners yesterday afternoon.'

'I heard about that,' said Grandpa Willy. 'They were all sick, weren't they? And they all had amnesia. Didn't even know what their own names were.'

'That's right. They were all suffering from RMSF . . . that's Rocky Mountain spotted fever. It can be pretty nasty if you don't treat it in time.'

'But you had some doxycycline,' said Jessica.

'Yes,' said Dr Leeming, in surprise. 'How do you know about doxycycline?'

Jessica didn't answer him, but went to the open door. She stared at Phoebe for a long time and then, when Phoebe eventually looked across at her, she said, 'Hello.'

Phoebe frowned. She didn't say anything and it was obvious to Jessica that she didn't know who she was.

'Are you better now?' Jessica asked her.

Phoebe nodded.

Jessica turned to Dr Leeming. 'How many others were there, apart from her?'

'Four – five altogether. We think they're all brothers and sisters. The police are trying to find their parents.'

'It's time for me to go now,' Jessica told Phoebe.

'Tickity-tock,' said Phoebe, and went back to watching television.

They drove back to the house through the softly falling snow. Grandpa Willy was chattering away as usual, but Jessica stayed silent. They passed the cemetery where the stone angel stood over the Pennington children's memorial. They passed Mrs Crawford's house, half buried in snow, and Jessica saw Mrs Crawford standing at her window, illuminated by orange firelight, just about to draw the curtains.

Mrs Crawford saw her and waved, but she didn't wave back.

In the kitchen, Grace was washing dishes and Epiphany was sitting at the kitchen table, braiding colored wool.

'Hi, Jessica, how you feeling?'

'I'm OK. Still got a headache.'

'That was a terrible thing that happened to you,' said Grace. 'Why, you could have been killed. I hope your grandpa takes that school for all the money they got.'

'I'm OK,' Jessica repeated. Then, to Epiphany, 'What are you making?'

'Tassels, to put in my hair. Beninese women believe that they keep away evil thoughts.'

'Piff—' said Jessica.

Epiphany stopped braiding and looked up at her.

'Nothing,' said Jessica. 'Just be careful crossing the road.'

As Jessica left the kitchen, Epiphany turned to Grace and pulled a bewildered face. 'Now what was that all about?'

In the back garden, cloven-footed in the snow, the statue of Pan looked slyly up at her bedroom window.

She tugged out her bed a little way. She had to see if there really was a stain on the wallpaper in the shape of a pig's head. But a large triangular piece of wallpaper had been torn away, so it was impossible to say.

She went up to the wall and pressed her hands against it. It was solid, and impenetrable. She tapped on it, and it sounded just like a wall, nothing else. She sat on her bed. She felt as if she were going mad. The girl in the dressing-table mirror looked back at her, white-faced, more like a ghost than a real girl.

On Monday, after Grandpa Willy had taken her to see Dr

Leeming for a check-up, she went back to school. She arrived in the middle of morning recess. Sue-Anne was sitting on her usual perch in the schoolyard, and there too were Renko and Elica and all her other cronies.

'Return of the gimp!' called Sue-Anne. 'Now showing in a schoolyard near you!'

Jessica stopped, holding her schoolbag close to her chest. Renko caught her looking at him and said, 'What's your problem, Gimpy?'

Jessica said, 'Nothing. I just wanted to thank you, that's all.'

'Thank me?' he snorted. 'What do you want to thank me for?'

'I want you to know that whatever part of you it was that came with me, and said that you liked me, and risked your life for me, I won't ever forget it, and I'll always be grateful.'

'The gimp finally flipped,' said Micky. 'That crack on the head must've been a real doozy.'

But for a flicker of a second Renko focused his gray eyes on her as if he could actually remember fighting with the wooden wolf, and crossing the painted lake, and helping her to run across the fields and deserts of Patternworld. Then he gave her a dismissive flap of his hand and turned away.

'You see how irresistible I am? Even the gimp's in love with me.'

Elica burst out laughing. 'She has scramble-egg brain.'

That evening she went up to her bedroom as soon as supper was over and drew pictures of the overgrown garden, the forest of hat-stands and the seashore where Phoebe had sat swinging her bare toes in the incoming tide. She could remember it all, every detail. She could remember the teaspoons flying like ducks in the sunset, and the trees made of black lace, and the stained-glass house with its cozy light inside.

She adjusted the lamp on her desk so that she could see better, and as she did so something glinted in the corner of the bedroom and caught her eye. She went over and picked it up, and it was the sapphire ring that Mrs Fellowes had given to Mrs Crawford when she was a girl, to prove that she was still inside the wallpaper.

Jessica stared at it for a long time, and then she slipped it onto her finger.